Jessie could see little more than the
outline of a man and two horses.

When the doctor opened the office door, light from
the lamp poured into the street. Jessie saw the limp
form of a man draped over one of the horses. She got
only a fleeting glimpse, for as she turned the light
struck her face and the newcomer loosed an angry
growl.

"Hell's bells!" he snarled. "You're that damn Starbuck
woman from out at Nate Wheeler's claim! It was you
that shot my partner, you dirty bitch!"

Whirling as he dropped the reins he was holding, the
man grabbed for the pistol holstered low on his hip.

At the man's first blasphemous shout, Jessie's hand
had begun moving toward her Colt. She drew and
fired. The newcomer's weapon barked, an instant echo
to Jessie's shot...

→◆→ WESLEY ELLIS ◆←←

LONE STAR

AND THE
GOLD MINE WAR

J.®

A JOVE BOOK

LONE STAR AND THE GOLD MINE WAR

A Jove Book / published by arrangement with
the author

PRINTING HISTORY
Jove edition / October 1985

ISBN: 0-515-08368-2

PRINTED IN THE UNITED STATES OF AMERICA

LONE STAR

AND THE
GOLD MINE WAR

Chapter 1

"I don't hear the wind whistling as sharply as it was a while ago," Jessie told Ki. "Maybe the storm's dying out."

"About time it did," Ki replied. He went to the nearest window and peered into the blackness. "It's too dark outside to see anything, but the rain's stopped. At least, it's not hitting the window now, and the boat's not pitching as badly as it was a little while ago."

Jessie glanced around the main salon of the *New Albion,* a coastal steamer that made weekly runs between San Francisco and Seattle-Tacoma. It was a big room, spanning the width of the vessel at its widest point. Jessie and Ki were traveling to San Francisco after two weeks in the high timber country of Oregon and Washington, where Jessie had gone on the yearly tour that was part of her routine in managing the far-flung Starbuck enterprises.

During most of the time they'd spent inland, moving between timber stands and sawmills, the weather had been reasonably dry for an autumn on the North Pacific Coast. Although showers had fallen almost every day, most had been brief and there'd even been a few days when the sun shone and warmed the air until the season seemed like a second summer.

By the time their inland trip ended, though, the long cycle of winter had begun. Rain had fallen without a break as the steamer threaded its way up the tortuous, island-studded inland passage and steamed most of the fifty miles through the Strait of Juan de Fuca. As they'd approached the mouth of the strait, the overcast had grown steadily heavier. Even before the big sidewheeler emerged into the ocean, the rain had begun falling constantly. Now they had only another day to pass before the ship docked at San Francisco.

Jessie surveyed the big salon, deserted except for her and Ki, and went on, "I was sure some of the other passengers would come in here after supper, but I suppose all of them have given in to the weather and gone to bed."

"I can't say I blame them," Ki replied. "Since we came out of the straits into the open sea we've had nothing but rain and cold wind."

"Yes," Jessie nodded. "It's even worse than the rainy days we had while we were in the timberlands."

Ki moved to the door that led to the deck. He opened it a crack, grimaced when a trickle of cold air hit his face, but pushed the door still farther open and looked out. Turning back to Jessie, he said, "Even if the rain's stopped, it's still windy and cloudy enough to hide the stars. Just the same, I think I'll go out and make a circle or two around the deck before it starts raining again."

"I'll go with you, Ki. I need to stretch my legs, too."

Ki pulled the door open completely and held it while Jessie went out, then followed her to the deck. They moved to the rail and looked out across the water, the wind moist on their faces. Heavy clouds hid the sky and all that was visible of the restless ocean were the ghostly crests of the whitecaps that stretched across the surface of the Pacific from the sides of the ship until they were lost in the shrouded darkness.

Jessie went on, "I'll be glad to get back to Texas and the Circle Star, Ki. At least when we're at home I don't feel

2

like I need scales, fins, and gills to survive."

Ki said good-humoredly, "I'll remind you of that the next time you get worried about there not being enough rain to fill the waterholes."

"You won't have to remind me," Jessie told him. "I'll always remember the ocean, and I'll enjoy thinking about it when we get home where we're warm and dry again." She shivered as a fresh gust of chilly night air rippled against her face.

"We'd better walk," Ki suggested. "Even the little bit of moving we can do on the deck will keep us warm."

They started walking toward the bow of the ship, moving carefully on the rain-slick deck toward the high hump of the ship's sidewheels, hearing the splash of the big paddles inside their housing as they churned through the water. A few steps took them beyond the last windows of the salon, and when they had passed through the rectangle of light that streamed through the panes, they were in almost total darkness.

When they neared the wheel-housing the paddle splashes grew louder, as did the rhythmic thumping of the engines in the hold below the deck. A few steps past the wheel-housing, Jessie and Ki sensed rather than heard the thuds made by the feet of two men who jumped from the top of the cabin onto the deck behind them.

They turned to locate the alien sound, and at that moment two others dropped from the top of the cabin to the deck in front of them. Even in the dim light, Jessie and Ki could see the silvery glow of the knives carried by the quartet closing in on them.

Both Jessie and Ki lived with the constant awareness that they walked with danger much of the time when they were away from the isolated safety of the Circle Star. Having faced similar situations before, they did not need to speak,

3

but moved with quick decisiveness to counter the surprise attack. Tacitly Ki knew that he would take the first two and Jessie would handle the ones in front.

Jessie had not strapped on her gunbelt before going to the dining salon for supper, but she'd learned enough about the Oriental art of unarmed combat to react almost as quickly as Ki. The two men heading toward her carried their knives low, the blades gleaming wickedly in the dim light.

Taking a step backward, Jessie lured the leading assailant to lurch forward, his arm advancing in a thrust. As he lunged with the glittering blade extended, she brought her left hand down on his wrist in a *sagatana* chop that sent the knife clattering to the deck, then whirled in a *heiken* blow with her stiffened right hand that went home on her attacker's ear.

Yowling in a hoarse scream, the man bent double. He let his knife fall to the deck and brought both hands up to his head as though they could shield his ruptured eardrum. Jessie saw at once that he would be out of the combat long enough to allow her to deal with the second assailant, who was still two steps away from her.

Ki did not wait for the two men who were approaching him to get within thrusting distance. He whirled in a *yoko-geri-keage* kick that caught the leader of the pair in the larynx, rupturing it and starting a stream of blood flowing down the man's throat. The thug cried a gargling yell and staggered back, dropping his weapon as he raised his hands to his neck to try to stem blood that was choking him.

Without wasting a second of the time that remained before the other thug reached him, Ki spun around to evade the oncoming man's outstretched blade. As he moved within arm's length of his attacker, Ki knocked the man's knife arm aside with his left forearm bent in a *jodan-uke* block and pulled the knife wielder's head down while lifting his

4

knee with a *hiza-geri* kick. The man's face smashed into Ki's knee with a crunch of bone. The thug collapsed groaning on the deck, his face crushed and bleeding.

Meanwhile, Jessie was closing in on the second man who had singled her out as his quarry. She swept into a *kakato* kick that sent his outstretched arm aside, and as he staggered forward, getting closer to her, she knocked his knife hand wide of her body with a *naka-uke* sweep of her left arm while battering the bridge of his nose with her right elbow in a *kiji* blow.

When the point of her bent elbow drove with shattering force into the face of the onrushing attacker, Jessie could hear the bridge of his nose crack and feel it give way under her blow. His cry of agony faded into a gasping sigh as the thin razor-sharp shards of broken bone from his crushed nose sliced into his brain. He sagged lifelessly to the deck, motionless.

Ki's first assailant was the only one of the quartet who was still on his feet. Though he was staggering and still clutching his throat from which gargling gasps came as he fought to breathe, Ki did not risk allowing the thug to recover. He took a single long step to reach the man and pushed him to the rail, then bent and lifted him by the ankles to boost him over the ship's side.

Without waiting to watch the thug splash into the water, Ki turned to Jessie. She'd backed warily away from the huddled forms of the two who'd singled her out as their quarry.

"Are you all right, Jessie?" he asked.

"Of course—thanks to your lessons." She indicated the three disabled thugs and went on, "I think two of them are dead, and the other one won't last much longer."

"If we leave them here, it's going to create a big stir and a lot of newspaper stories when we get to San Francisco,"

5

he said thoughtfully. "What do you think, Jessie?"

"I'm not feeling very merciful right now."

Ki indicated the ocean's billowing waves with his head and asked, "Over the side, then?"

"Yes," Jessie replied decisively. "There's no doubt in my mind who sent them after us."

"Nor in mine," he answered. "The cartel, of course."

Jessie nodded. "One of the cartel bosses must have seen that interview in the *Tacoma Times*. I didn't want to talk to the reporter, but he backed me into a corner."

Ki was already dragging the thug who was still alive toward the rail. He lifted the man and let him drop into the heaving ocean, then hoisted the lifeless bodies of the other two over the rail and let them join their companions in the turbulent water.

Jessie said, "We'll have to report this to the captain, Ki. If we don't, there'll be a big uproar when the ship docks in San Francisco and they're not checked off the passenger list."

"Won't there be as much of an uproar when the captain reports that they attacked us?"

"Not if we handle things right," Jessie said slowly, her voice thoughtful. "Let's go back to the salon where we'll be warm. We need to think about this for a few minutes before we report it to the captain. I'm sure he's never heard of the cartel; few people have."

Few people, indeed, in the bustling United States of the late nineteenth century were aware of the existence of the sinister European cartel that was attempting to take over the prospering nation's key industries. Jessie's father, Alex Starbuck, had been one of the few and Alex had dedicated his life to thwarting the cartel's scheme.

Jessie went on, "The captain will accept what's happened as an attempt to rob us if we just give him a bare-bones

6

story and avoid going into too many details. Then we'll cut our stay in San Francisco down to just a couple of days and hurry home to the Circle Star."

To Jessie, as it had been to her father, the huge sprawling ranch in sparsely populated southwestern Texas was a treasured home. The Circle Star covered more than three hundred sections, each section a square mile of land, and it sprawled over parts of three Texas counties, making the ranch larger than most working cattle spreads and even larger than some small nations in Europe.

Alex Starbuck had created the Circle Star as an isolated and peaceful haven, where he could go to rest from his continuing battles with agents of the cartel. Ironically, the very isolation of the Circle Star and the broken terrain of parts of its boundaries had made it hard to defend. A murderous band of merciless assassins hired by the cartel had swooped in a surprise raid onto the Circle Star, and Alex had died in a hail of their bullets.

Through his unaided efforts before his untimely death, Jessie's father had created an industrial empire. Starting with a small store in San Francisco, dealing with Oriental curios and art objects, Alex had used his business acumen to prosper. As his business grew, he'd bought a rusting, battered merchant ship to transport his merchandise from Japan and China.

To make the return voyages to the Orient profitable, Alex had sought export cargoes in the United States, and within a short time his lone ship had earned enough to make possible the purchase of a second and then a third ship. Soon Alex found himself heading a major shipping line. Then the need to replace his aging vessels had led him to use his profits to found his own shipyard, where he could supervise the details of the vessels under construction.

In the space of the next few years, the Starbuck enterprises had prospered and expanded under Alex's shrewd guidance. The shipyard had attracted his interest to the raw materials it required, which led Alex to become interested in setting up a foundry to produce steel plates for ship hulls and timberlands to provide the lumber required for the finished vessels.

With the flowering of the railroad age, Alex had kept his foundry busy turning out rails as well as steel plates. The increasing need for iron ore led to the acquisition of interests in mining, and copper and gold mines were soon added to those producing ferrous ores. His virtually unbroken record of successes attracted the attention not only of the industrial world, but of the men who managed business finances.

As his reputation for business acumen and strong management grew, Alex no longer needed to look for fresh ventures. He was invited by financiers to join them in forming new banks and brokerage houses. The demands on his time that these basically more important interests created ultimately led him to training good men to handle the actual operating details of his widely scattered enterprises and to concentrate largely on the financial aspects that were so important to keeping his empire healthy.

Alex's name became well-known not only in the booming United States, but in economically foundering Europe. He was invited to join a European group, ostensibly another business venture. Alex had learned by experience to investigate any offers he received. In this case, his private investigation of the group's members revealed to him that they had a secret objective: to form a cartel which by any methods, legal or illicit, would transfer the control of key American enterprises to a small circle of European nobility and bankers.

Alex had refused to become part of the cartel. Realizing

that he had learned too many of their secrets, the merciless cartel's members set out to discredit Alex and break him in the marketplace. When their efforts to do this failed, the cartel hired killers to murder him, and though earlier efforts were thwarted by the vigilance of Alex and Ki, the cartel's plotters eventually succeeded in bringing about Alex's untimely death.

Jessie had inherited her father's strength and abilities as well as his enemies. After she'd recovered from the shock of Alex's murder, she took up the active management of the industrial and financial empire she'd inherited. As soon as she had satisfied herself that the managers chosen by Alex were going to work with her as diligently as they had with her dead father, Jessie also took up Alex's battle against the cartel.

In this she was aided and supported by Ki, who had been Alex's strong right hand for several years. The son of a Japanese mother and an American father, Ki had been driven from his own home by the stubborn anti-American prejudice of his mother's parents. Embittered by the treatment he and his mother had received from her tradition-imprisoned family, Ki soon left Japan and traveled to the United States, seeking to make a new life for himself.

When Ki abandoned his homeland and came to America, his only contact had been the old and trusted friend of his father: Alex Starbuck. At the time of Ki's arrival, Alex was still trying to recover from shock at the death of his wife, Jessie's mother, but this had not kept him from welcoming Ki.

Taking Ki into his home, Alex treated him like a son. Although Ki's anger and sorrow did not diminish, Alex and Jessie had become the family of which Ki had been deprived. After Alex's murder, Ki had remained at Jessie's side, joining her in the battle she took up against the cartel, protecting her with his mastery of Oriental martial arts, which he'd learned under the tutelage of the great warrior-teacher, Hirata.

Now, walking beside Jessie along the mist-shrouded deck of the *New Albion,* Ki said, "I'll stay in the background as much as possible while you talk to the captain, Jessie. He may share some of the unfortunate attitude toward Orientals that we sometimes run into in California."

Jessie nodded absently, her mind busy thinking of the best way to tell their story to the ship's captain. They reached the door of the salon and went in, finding it still deserted.

"We'll have to take it for granted that the men who attacked us were cartel operatives, Ki," she began.

"Of course," he nodded. "They couldn't be anything else. We've already agreed to that."

"There's no reason to take the captain into our confidence, though," Jessie went on. "We'll simply say they attacked us and that we assume they were trying to rob us."

"Which is quite probably true," Ki nodded. "I'm sure they would have taken our money if they'd succeeded in killing us."

"There's no point in delaying our visit to the captain, then," Jessie said. "It'll be an unpleasant job at best, so let's go find him and get it over with."

Jessie and Ki wasted no time retracing their steps to the main salon and went through the big room to the opposite side of the vessel, where the captain's office was located. Ki looked questioningly at Jessie before he knocked at the door marked CAPTAIN CARL OLSEN. She nodded and he tapped lightly with his knuckles, iron-hard due to the rigorous routine he followed to keep himself in top condition for the blows used in unarmed combat.

"Please to come in," a slightly accented baritone voice responded to the knock.

Ki opened the door and stood aside for Jessie to enter.

The captain of the *New Albion* had started rising to his feet when he saw her, and now he made a stiffly formal bow in European style. Jessie looked at him with very little effort to disguise her curiosity. This was the second time she'd seen the captain. The first was a brief glimpse when he'd bowed to her after a hurried introduction on deck by the purser during the bustle of boarding at Tacoma.

Jessie had been too preoccupied to do more than return the captain's bow with a nod, and she saw now that he was unexpectedly young to be in command of a ship such as the *New Albion*. She judged him to be in his early thirties. He was a tall man, broad-shouldered, with dark blond hair and the fleshy nose, wide cheekbones, and square jaw that spoke of Scandinavian ancestry. He studied Jessie with ice-blue eyes during the moment she spent looking at him, and he was the first to speak.

"Miss Starbuck," he said. His words had the faintest touch of his native tongue, an almost imperceptible accent, and as he went on his phrasing now and then showed the strangely formal construction used by those who may have learned English late in life. He went on, "I regret that I haven't paid my respects to you before now. Please, sit down." He motioned to the chair across the desk from his own, then belatedly turned to Ki. "Please, you will take a chair also, Mr.—"

"Ki. And without any title, if you don't mind, Captain," Ki replied, settling into one of the chairs that stood against the wall.

"Yes, to be sure. Only Ki," Olsen nodded. He returned his attention to Jessie. "Please, Miss Starbuck, you will understand that it is not of my own choice that I have not been able to welcome you on board the *New Albion* before now. The bad weather has kept me on the bridge most of the time."

"Of course, I understand, Captain," Jessie said when he

11

paused. "But I'm afraid we have something worse than weather to tell you about."

"What could be worse than the weather?" Olsen asked.

"Attempted robbery," Jessie said flatly. "And for all Ki and I know, perhaps attempted murder."

Chapter 2

Captain Olsen's jaw dropped and he stared at Jessie, disbelief showing in his face. Then he asked, "You are telling me that one of your fellow passengers has tried to steal from you, perhaps to kill you?"

"I'm not sure whether they were passengers—" Jessie began, then stopped as Olsen broke in.

"You say 'they.' There were more robbers than one, then?" he asked.

"There were four of them," she replied.

"Four robbers?" Olsen asked, his voice registering his incredulity. "And did they have weapons?"

"Yes," Jessie nodded. "All four had knives."

"Please, you will relate to me what has happened, Miss Starbuck, and describe to me these men as best you can," Olsen said, a frown forming on his face as he spoke. "I will then take quick steps to see that the scoundrels who tried to steal from you are hunted down and captured."

"That won't be necessary, Captain," Jessie began. "You see, Ki and I—"

Olsen broke in. "Ah! You and your—your aide, you have taken them already prisoners, then?"

"Not exactly," Jessie replied. She paused for a moment to choose her words carefully so that she would be telling the literal truth, then went on, "They went overboard into the water as a result of the fight we had with them."

13

For the second time the captain stared agape at Jessie. He swallowed and brought his lips together as he studied her slight figure and then turned his gaze to Ki, who had not stirred since sitting down. Then Olsen shook his head.

"I do not wish to offend you, Miss Starbuck," he said. "But I find it hard to believe what you have told me."

Her voice cold, Jessie said, "I've told you the facts, Captain Olsen. Whether you believe them or not—"

Olsen broke in hastily. "I do not question the truth of what you say, Miss Starbuck. I only am trying to understand how you and—and Ki defeated four armed men unless you also had weapons. Do you carry firearms? For if you do, you must surely have been told when your tickets you purchased that any guns brought aboard the *New Albion* by a passenger must be given at once into the care of the purser."

"We weren't armed, Captain Olsen," Jessie said. "And Ki and I didn't buy tickets ourselves; they were bought for us by a clerk in the Tacoma office of one of my lumber mills."

"Ah," Olsen nodded. Then he frowned again. "If you had no weapons, Miss Starbuck, please relate to me how you and Ki managed to defeat these four men you say attacked you."

"Ki has great skill in—" Jessie hesitated as she tried to summon up the best and most easily understood definition of Ki's martial arts skills. She went on, "Great skill in the Oriental method of unarmed combat."

"Ah," Olsen repeated. "I have seen such skill demonstrated when I visited the Far East. You speak of Tae Kwon Do?"

For the first time Ki felt called on to take part in the conversation. "That is only one branch of the skill Miss Starbuck means, Captain Olsen," he volunteered. "There are others as well. I have some knowledge of most of them."

"Obviously enough to defeat four men armed with knives,"

14

Olsen said. "To me, that would mean that your skill is very great, Ki."

"It was enough to save our lives when the thugs attacked us," Jessie said quickly. "I'm sure you'll agree that we were forced to defend ourselves, Captain."

"Certainly," Olsen nodded, then went on, "and you defended yourselves so effectively that the four men who tried to rob you are now at the bottom of the sea."

"Unfortunately, that's true," Jessie agreed.

"You did not recognize them?" Olsen asked.

Jessie shook her head. "It was dark on the deck. But I'm sure we hadn't seen the men before, Captain. Of course, the bad weather's kept most of the passengers in their cabins."

Olsen nodded. "Yes, I can understand that in the dark you would not be able to tell whether you had seen them before. But I'm sure you realize, Miss Starbuck, this is a very serious matter for me. Not only to the owners of the *New Albion,* but to the Coast Guard of the United States, I am accountable for everything that happens aboard my ship."

"Believe me, Captain Olsen, I consider this as just as serious as you do," Jessie replied coldly. "Remember, we were attacked by those men."

"If I have offended you, Miss Starbuck, I most sincerely apologize," Olsen said. "I am only trying to find out the facts of this affair."

"Ki and I certainly don't want to hinder you, Captain," Jessie said. "In fact, we want to help you. We'd like to know if these thugs were passengers and where they got on board."

"I will be able to tell you that after the purser checks the passenger lists to find out who is missing," Olsen told Jessie. "And when we put in at San Francisco, there will certainly be an official hearing required by your Coast Guard."

"We won't delay you any longer, then," Jessie said. She

15

stood up. "You'll find us in our cabins or in the main salon when you have something to tell us," she said as she and Ki exited.

"You walked a tightrope very nicely, Jessie," Ki observed while they walked along the deck toward their staterooms. "What do you expect the captain will find out?"

"I'm sure he'll learn that no passengers are missing, Ki," Jessie replied. "My guess is that those four men came aboard at Astoria. There'd have been plenty of time for their orders to be telegraphed from Tacoma or Seattle. And I don't imagine they'd have bothered to buy tickets."

Ki nodded. "With all the confusion at the docks, it'd be easy enough for them to pose as longshoremen. All they'd need to do would be to pick up a box or something and carry it into the hold."

"We'll know soon enough," Jessie said. "Captain Olsen was certainly in a hurry to get his own investigation started. It's going to take the purser quite a while to check the passengers, though, so I don't think we'll hear from him until tomorrow."

Jessie's prediction proved correct. She and Ki were sitting at their breakfast in the dining salon the following morning when Captain Olsen stopped at their table.

He indicated the empty chair across from Jessie and asked, "Would you very much mind if I joined you, Miss Starbuck?"

"We'd be delighted, Captain," she replied. "Please do."

Olsen settled into the chair and a steward hurried to the table carrying a cup of coffee. Waiting until the man had left, the captain said, "Last night the purser verified that all the passengers listed on our manifest are safely on board, Miss Starbuck."

"I was sure that would be the case," Jessie nodded.

"As a second precaution, I also instructed the mate to search the cargo hold," Olsen went on. "His men discovered

16

that a number of crates had been moved around to make a place on the lower deck where four men could hide. There was some food left in the space he found."

"Then you must have reached the same conclusion that Ki and I did," Jessie said. "Those men could have intended to rob other passengers as well, then sneak off the ship when it docked in San Francisco."

Nodding agreement, the captain said, "To think so is most logical." He paused to sip his coffee, then went on, "Now, I have something to tell you of which you may not be aware, Miss Starbuck. I hope you will understand that I am not speaking for myself or for this ship's owners."

"You sound very serious, Captain," Jessie said.

"I assure you that it is very serious to me," Olsen nodded. "I wished to explain why this is so, before you are served with the subpoena to testify."

"Subpoena?" Jessie frowned. "Testify? That sounds like you're talking about a trial, Captain Olsen."

"Not a trial," the captain said. "An inquiry made by the Coast Guard whenever a passenger is lost overboard from a ship in United States's waters. As soon as I make my report, you and Ki will receive subpoenas to appear as witnesses."

"All we could say is that we were attacked by four men and that they went overboard as a result of the fight we had with them," Jessie frowned.

"That is the most important thing," Olsen told her. "And I would not expect you to say more."

"Wouldn't the Coast Guard accept your testimony?"

"This inquiry is to discover if lives were lost through any fault or mistake of mine, or through any defect, short-coming, or flaw in the structure of the *New Albion*," Olsen explained.

"I'm afraid I don't follow you," Jessie frowned.

"If I should be found at fault, it could damage or perhaps

even put an end to my professional career. If the blame is placed on the owners, a very large fine could be levied against them."

"Of course, I can understand your concern, now," Jessie nodded. "But how long will this hearing last? I hadn't planned to stay in San Francisco more than two or three days."

"What happened is very clear, and in my opinion there is no question of a command fault or structural flaw, so it should take only a few hours," Olsen assured her. "And it will be called without any delay. We will dock in San Francisco early tomorrow, and I will make my report to the Coast Guard at once. The hearing will probably be held the next morning. I do not know what your plans are, but they should not be too greatly disturbed."

"From what you've said, I don't really have much choice about testifying, do I?" Jessie asked.

Olsen shook his head. "The Coast Guard has the authority to compel you to appear and testify, Miss Starbuck. But I'm sure the owners of the *New Albion* would wish me to be helpful to you in any way possible."

"Well, I appreciate your interest, Captain," Jessie said. "But if the hearing is held immediately, testifying won't be any real inconvenience."

"I am very glad to hear you say that," Olsen nodded. He started to continue, stopped and studied Jessie's face for two or three seconds, then went on, "I hope you will not think me too forward, Miss Starbuck, but would you do me the honor of dining with me tomorrow evening?" He continued quickly, "I do not mean dinner on board. We will dock early in the morning, and my duties should be ended by late afternoon, certainly in time for us to sit down at dinner at a reasonable hour."

"Why—" Jessie hid her surprise at Olsen's unexpected invitation. She gazed at him for a moment, suddenly aware that too long a time had passed since she'd dined alone with

18

a man and with characteristic quickness made a decision. She went on, "I think I'd enjoy that very much, Captain."

"I am honored, Miss Starbuck," Olsen said. "And since my time must be devoted to my ship entirely tomorrow, it will be better if we agree on a time when I will call for you."

"Eight o'clock, do you think?" Jessie asked. "You should be through by then. Ki and I will be at the Palace Hotel."

"I also stop there when I must stay longer than overnight in San Francisco," the captain said. "And although the Palm Court chef is very good, the Cliff House occurs to me as a suitable place for dinner unless you're tired of looking at the ocean."

"Oh, I always enjoy eating there," Jessie replied.

"Then it is settled," Olsen said, standing up. "Now, I must go and attend to my duties, Miss Starbuck. Until tomorrow evening, then."

Ki waited until the captain was out of earshot before he turned to Jessie and said, "I'm glad you accepted the captain's invitation. We're running short of some kitchen supplies for the main house, things I can only get in Chinatown. I was wondering how I'd find time to buy them since we're going to be in San Francisco such a short time."

"After eating in logging camps for the past several weeks, it'll at least be a change," she observed. "And I'm sure that the captain will be good company on shore, where he doesn't have a ship on his mind."

"I hope you're not worrying about your appearance at the Coast Guard hearing tomorrow," Captain Olsen said to Jessie as the hackney cab started down Market Street for the long ride to the Cliff House.

"All that I can do is testify as to what happened," Jessie replied. "Since Ki and I were acting in self-defense, I assume there isn't any reason for me to worry."

19

"A very sensible attitude indeed," he said. "You are quite a remarkable woman, Miss Starbuck."

"Since we're going to have dinner together, don't you think we can be less formal?" Jessie suggested. "If you would call me Jessie—"

"And you call me Carl—" the captain chimed in. He chuckled. "That will make our evening more pleasant, of course." He was silent for a moment, but then went on, "I'm greatly pleased that you accepted my invitation, Jessie, and to be truthful, I'm also a bit surprised."

"Why surprised, Carl?" she asked. "You and I are in very much the same situation, when you stop to think about it."

"How do you arrive at that conclusion?"

Jessie could hear in Olsen's voice the frown that she could not see on his face in the darkness of the cab. She replied, "Both of us live in isolation. I spend most of my time at the Circle Star, my ranch in Texas. The nearest town is a two-day horseback ride and my closest neighbor's ranch is a dozen miles away. You spend most of your time on your ship, where I'm sure your position must isolate you from the crew and passengers."

"Strange," Olsen said thoughtfully. "I hadn't looked at it in that light before, but it's quite true. I'm seldom lucky enough to enjoy an evening like this one, with a woman who's both wise and charming."

Jessie was far from being unaccustomed to compliments of the sort Carl Olsen had paid her. In her teens, Alex Starbuck had placed her in the charge of Myobu, a wise old geisha; to be instructed in the relationships between men and women, and the old woman had done her work well. When in her maturity Jessie traveled the path that leads quickly from introduction to intimacy, her early lessons stood her in good stead.

Thanks to her training, Jessie had learned to recognize in a quick glance the self-seeking Don Juans who were searching only for fresh conquests to boast about and men who were genuinely lonely and would value her for herself. As she'd grown older, Jessie had developed her own sure instincts, which supplemented the geisha's training. She wisely chose partners with whom to share the physical relationships about which she had learned in her lessons from Myobu.

As the cab rolled through the darkness toward Seal Point and the Cliff House, Jessie needed little reflection to conclude that Carl Olsen was a man who met her requirements as a lover. She also recognized the strain of shyness that lay behind his formal manners and decided that she would give him any further encouragement he might need.

She turned toward him, her face a pale oval in the shadow, and asked in a lightly joking tone, "Then you aren't like the sailors we hear about so much, Carl? You don't have a girl in every port?"

"I stay in most ports only overnight," Olsen replied. "And my time I generally spend with my ship. I'm always too busy to think of anything except getting ready to sail again."

Careful to keep her voice light and half-joking, Jessie said, "You know what they say about all work and no play."

"It makes Jack a dull boy," Olsen replied. "Do you find me dull, then, Jessie?"

"No, indeed. I think you're a very charming man."

"I am complimented, Jessie." Somewhat clumsily, Olsen groped for Jessie's hand and raised it until he could bend and touch it lightly with his lips. He said, "You are perhaps—"

Whatever he planned to say further was lost as the hackman turned the carriage into the half-moon drive that led to the short walkway of the Cliff House and reined in.

There was a crowd in the popular restaurant, and an attentive waiter, who hovered close to their table, inhibited personal conversation. Jessie, fresh from the beef dishes

21

served in the lumber camps and accustomed to eating steak twice a day at the Circle Star, suggested that they confine the meal to the seafood in which the Cliff House specialized.

In his ordering, Captain Olsen showed a gourmet's touch, which she found very pleasing and appealing. Their dinner proved to be one which could have been enjoyed nowhere except in the area around San Francisco Bay.

They began with two specialties particular to the region, tiny bay shrimp, smaller than the tip of Jessie's little finger, served in a mildly spiced sauce, followed by bowls of cioppino, a light stew of fish and shellfish found only in the bay and its nearby ocean waters. For the main course, there was *langouste,* the clawless lobster of the Pacific, prepared in a Chinese style with sweet and sour sauce that contained small shreds of pork as tender and white as the flesh of the shellfish itself.

To go with their dinner, the captain ordered a bottle of wine made from Reisling-type green Hungarian grapes, which came from the Buena Vista winery founded by an early Californian vintner, Anton Hazdrathy. With their dessert he called for a split of Mumm's *Cordon Rouge.*

"You've given me one of the most delicious meals I've had in years, Carl," Jessie told her host as they settled back into the hackney cab for the ride back to town.

"I'm pleased that you enjoyed it," Olsen replied. "Doubly pleased, because it encourages me to ask if you will dine with me again tomorrow night."

"You're sure that your ship won't need all your attention after the hearing?"

Olsen took Jessie's hand, and this time he did not hesitate to bring it to his lips. "For you, I will put duty in second place," he said. "This has been such an evening as I enjoy all too seldom. I hate to see it so near the end."

Jessie decided that the time had come for her to take the plunge she'd been debating for the past hour. Turning her

22

face up to her companion, she said in a half whisper, "It doesn't have to end until you choose, Carl. And how it ends will be your choice as well."

"You know the choice I'll make, Jessie," Olsen said as he bent to kiss her.

Jessie returned the kiss with fervor, and as the hackney rumbled over the dark Point Lobos Road toward the heart of the city, Olsen's lips moved from her lips to her slim neck and over her soft shoulders to the cleft between her breasts where they protruded above her low-cut dress. The gravel-covered road gave way to pavement when the hack reached Geary Street and the glow of the first gas streetlight flashed into the carriage.

"No more now, Carl," Jessie whispered, lifting Olsen's head. "We'll be at the hotel in a few minutes, alone. Then we can be together without worrying about a hackman who might turn to look at us any minute or about prying eyes glimpsing us from the street."

Chapter 3

Before the sharp metallic clicking of his room's lock had died away, Carl Olsen turned to Jessie and took her in his arms. She raised her face and he bent to kiss her lips. They held their embrace, bodies pressed close, tongues meeting in the darting, twining stabs of a passionate kiss. Then Jessie felt the bulge of Olsen's erection pressing against her thigh. She let one arm fall from his neck and dropped her hand to his groin to caress him with her soft fingertips.

Olsen quivered and she felt his muscles contract as he began to pull her closer to him. Breaking their kiss, Jessie said, "We're still too far apart, Carl. The bed's waiting for us right across the room."

"I want you now!" he replied. "I must have you without waiting, Jessie!"

"I feel the same way," she breathed softly. "There'll be plenty of time for the bed. Let go of me for just a moment."

Reluctantly, Olsen released Jessie from his arms. She slid her hand into the placket of her dress and quickly undid the two buttons around her slim waist. Letting her filmy underpants drop to the floor, Jessie stepped away from them and lifted her full skirt.

Olsen gasped as he saw the symmetrical fullness of her marble-white thighs and the dark blond triangle at their apex. He kept his eyes fixed on her while his hands darted quickly to the fly of his trousers. Jessie's eyes widened as she saw the length and thickness of his liberated shaft spring up when his trousers slid down his thighs. Aware that she was already moist, she turned and bent forward.

"Your waiting's over, Carl," she said. "I'm as ready as you are!"

Olsen needed no second invitation. Jessie felt his warm hands grasp her hips. She spread her legs wider, bent down a bit more, then drew her breath sharply as her lover went into her with a single long thrust. She sighed as he began stroking fiercely with short thrusts and tightened her inner muscles to intensify the sensation that after her long abstinence was beginning to affect her more quickly than usual.

Suddenly Olsen gasped and the tempo of his thrusts quickened momentarily before she felt him begin to quiver. He stopped stroking and pressed himself hard against her. Jessie felt him fading and her sensations died away as well.

Olsen sighed deeply and said in a half whisper, "Forgive me for stopping, Jessie," he said. "It has been so long."

"Don't worry, Carl," Jessie told him as he moved away from her. "We have the whole night ahead of us."

"But you—"

Turning to face him, Jessie held out her arms. After hesitating for a moment, Olsen stepped closer to her, his movements hampered by the trousers that had fallen to a crumpled heap at his ankles. Jessie took him in her arms and he buried his face into the softness of her shoulder.

Her voice soft, Jessie whispered, "I understand more than you might think, Carl. But we don't have to worry about the time or anything else. Let's finish undressing now and have a warm bath before we go to bed."

They undressed as new lovers have since time's beginning, helping one another, pausing for quick kisses and small caresses, while the big marble tub in the bathroom was filling with hot water. Like almost everything else in the new hotel, the tub seemed larger than life, big enough to accommodate both of them easily. For a half hour they splashed and soaped and rinsed, then as the water began to cool, they dried on fleecy towels and started for the bed, twined in an embrace.

Jessie had counted on the bath to overcome her partner's embarrassment, but in spite of her caresses and the almost constant contact of their bodies in the tub, Olsen was still flaccid. She waited for him to lie down, then stretched out beside him. He sought her lips, and she began stroking and fondling his half-inert shaft with her fingertips while their tongues entwined in long lingering kisses, and she continued her attentions when Olsen broke their kiss. He dropped his head to her breasts and started to rasp his tongue over the protruding pink tips that the bath had brought to bud in the center of her breasts.

After a few moments, Jessie stirred. She sat up, and when Olsen looked up at her with an unhappy frown, she said, "Lie quietly, Carl. I'm not going to leave you."

She bent to kiss Olsen's eyes and pressed a hand over them as she brushed her lips lightly over his. Then she started placing soft fleeting kisses down his neck and chest and over his flat muscled torso until she reached his crotch. Lifting his flaccid shaft, she rubbed her cheeks across its tip for several minutes before dropping her head to his groin. The layered muscles of his abdomen rippled and grew taut as Jessie slowly trailed a string of tongue-flicking kisses from the base of his burgeoning sex to the tip.

When she felt him beginning to swell in response to her gentle caresses, Jessie engulfed his beginning erection and closed her lips around it. Then she stroked the tender tip firmly and slowly with her agile tongue. Olsen's body was taut now, and his shaft swelled further as Jessie continued her expert attentions. She waited until he'd grown completely erect, then released him and stretched out beside him.

Olsen moved quickly. He rose to his knees and slid between Jessie's outspread thighs while she guided his shaft

26

to the moist nest that was waiting for him. He went into her with a single, long, deliberate penetration that Jessie thought would never end, nor did she want it to. Already roused by the caresses she'd used in restoring his erection, Jessie moaned happily as she finally felt his swollen cylinder of firm flesh fill her to the utmost. For a few moments she lay motionless, her head arched back, rotating her hips slowly to increase the sensation that had started sending short involuntary shudders sweeping over her.

When Olsen bent forward and his lips sought hers, Jessie returned his kiss with a darting tongue that was matched by the fervor of her lover's. While their tongues entwined he began driving into her with long measured lunges that soon brought her to a writhing, trembling response. Locking her ankles together, Jessie matched his deliberate thrusts by lifting her hips and letting them fall in rhythm with his long, slow strokes.

Minutes ticked off while the pair swayed in unison until the climax that Jessie had been forced to postpone took her with a sudden unexpected wave and she cried out with delight. Olsen kept thrusting with growing fervor, while Jessie trembled through a series of fading ripples of satisfaction. Then, as he gave no sign of tiring, she caught and matched his rhythm once again. She raised her hips lustily, twisting them in unison with his fierce downward lunges, increasing the rippling ecstasy of returning pleasure that was again beginning to sweep through her body.

Time did not seem to pass, and their passionate embrace was prolonged until Jessie felt herself mounting to another climax. Olsen was thrusting with a quicker rhythm now, and she could tell that he was also on the verge once more. She held her urge in check until her lover began gasping and his lunges increased to triphammer speed and force.

When Olsen uttered a final climactic gasp and she felt his body start to quiver uncontrollably, Jessie released her firm control. Together they swept into the final seconds of

27

their embrace. Pleasure mounted to an unbearable peak and passed it. The total relaxation of passion's ebb overtook them both; they lay still and spent.

After a long while, Jessie whispered, "You're a marvelous lover, Carl."

"I'm glad I please you, Jessie. For a while—"

Jessie placed her forefinger across his lips. "Hush," she said. "All that matters is that we're both happy, and that the night's still got a long way to go. Now, kiss me again. I don't want to waste a minute of the night before we have to say good morning."

To the relief of both Jessie and Ki, the hearing at Coast Guard headquarters the following morning was brief and formal, almost perfunctory. After calling Olsen to the witness stand to verify the approximate location of the *New Albion* and the weather conditions at the time of the attack on Jessie and Ki, the presiding officer called Jessie to the stand.

"Miss Starbuck," he began, "we've already established that the night when this incident occurred was dark and the seas were rough. Now I'd like for you to describe briefly in your own words what happened when you and your aide were attacked."

"There was enough light for us to see that all four of the men who jumped off the top of the cabins were armed with knives," Jessie began. "Ki is skilled in the Oriental methods of hand-to-hand fighting, and he's taught me a bit of it. We could see at once that our only hope was to back up to the rail and keep any of them from getting behind us. They rushed at us, and we fought back. I can't say exactly what moves each of us made, for everything happened very quickly. I'm sure the actual fight lasted only a minute or even less. When it was over, all four men had fallen or been thrown over the rail into the water."

28

"And neither of you was harmed?" the Coast Guardsman asked.

"No. We managed to dodge or parry their knives."

"Your description's been very clear, Miss Starbuck," the Coast Guard officer said thoughtfully. "It's quite obvious to anyone who's familiar with the Starbuck name that neither you nor your companion would have had reason to be the aggressor." He paused for a moment, then asked, "In your opinion, Miss Starbuck, do you feel that Captain Olsen or his officers were in any way negligent in allowing these men who attacked you to board the *New Albion* without being detected?"

"Of course not," Jessie replied. "Anyone who's boarded a ship has seen how hurried and bustling things are at a dock where the ship is being loaded or unloaded. I'm sure that if I were to set my mind to it, I'd have no trouble sneaking aboard a vessel without being noticed."

After a moment of thoughtful silence, the Coast Guardsman looked at Ki and asked, "Is there anything you would like to add to Miss Starbuck's testimony?"

Without rising from his seat in the front row of the chairs reserved for witnesses or others participating in the hearing, Ki shook his head.

"Then I'm going to declare this matter closed," the officer went on. "With no blame assessed and no charges brought against Miss Starbuck or her companion. Nor will any blame be assessed against the owners of the *New Albion,* or Captain Carl Olsen, or any member of his crew. This hearing stands adjourned."

As Jessie and Ki reached the door of the hearing room, Carl Olsen hurried from his seat to join them. He said, "Thank you, Jessie. I'm sure my owners will be as grateful as I am for what you said on the witness stand."

"I just explained what happened," Jessie replied. "And I certainly don't expect any credit for that."

After a quick glance at Ki, who'd stopped a few steps away when Olsen reached Jessie's side, the captain dropped his voice and went on, "I have much more to thank you for than what you said on the stand. Can I do that during dinner tonight?"

"Of course," Jessie replied. "And after dinner as well, if you wish."

"I'll call for you at seven, then," Olsen said.

"And I'll be waiting," she promised.

Olsen turned to go and Jessie rejoined Ki, who had just flagged down a passing hackney. He handed Jessie into the cab and settled into the seat across from her.

"Where shall I tell the cabbie to take us, Jessie?" he asked. "To the hotel? Or somewhere else?"

"Just tell him to start toward Montgomery Street, Ki. I have a few business calls that I want to make this morning."

Ki passed on the instructions to the hackman and turned back to Jessie. "Will you want me to go with you?"

"I don't see why you should, Ki. I'm just going to take care of a few routine things," she replied. "I'll have to drop in at Frank Allison's office. He should have the papers for that timberland lease I arranged in Spokane ready for me to sign. And since the bank is on the way to Frank's office, it'll be a good time to pay Walter Edmonds a courtesy call."

"There's nothing you'll need me for at the lawyer's office or the bank," Ki said. "So I'll ride with you as far as Montgomery, and while you're making your calls I'll walk to Kearney and finish my shopping. Shall I come back to the hotel when I'm through?"

"Not unless you want to. This afternoon I intend to do a little shopping at the City of Paris."

"I'll take my time, then," Ki nodded. "And when I finish, I'll go back to the hotel. If you're still planning on starting home tomorrow, I can pick up our tickets."

"Of course, we're starting home," Jessie replied. "You know how I miss the Circle Star, Ki. I want to ride and work with the hands shaping up the market herd."

"I'll get the tickets, then," Ki said. "And we'll be back at the ranch in plenty of time."

Jessie and Ki parted in front of the First California Bank building, a handsome three-story structure of cut stone. The bank was one in which Alex had acquired a controlling interest in the early days when he was expanding his financial empire. The doorman bowed her into the marble-floored lobby and she crossed it to the mahogany counter that enclosed the officers's desks. Walter Edmonds, the president, saw her coming and hurried to the railing to greet her.

"Jessie!" he exclaimed. "This is a pleasant surprise. I had no idea you were here in San Francisco. Let's go into my private office where we can talk."

"I just stopped in to say hello," Jessie protested, "not for a long visit."

"Just the same, if you can spare a few minutes, I'd like to talk privately with you," Edmonds said. "I've been debating overnight whether to send you a telegram at the Circle Star, or write a letter that would allow me to go into greater detail."

"If you were thinking about wiring me, you must have a real problem," Jessie commented as Edmonds escorted her into a large walnut-paneled office that opened off the enclosed area. He pulled a chair up to his desk and Jessie sat down. She went on, "I hope it isn't with the federal bank examiners."

"It doesn't have any direct connection with the bank," Edmonds assured her. "But it does affect the farmlands you own in the Sacramento and San Joaquin Valleys."

"Lease adjustments, I suppose?"

Edmonds shook his head. "No. Lease cancellations."

"But all the farmers renting Starbuck land seemed to be satisfied with the lease revisions we made last year," Jessie frowned. "Why have they changed their minds?"

"They're afraid conditions in the valleys will change," Edmonds replied. "It's not a case of dissatisfaction, Jessie. This is much more serious. Unless you or someone else steps in to stop what's about to happen, your land in those valleys and perhaps the valleys themselves are going to be turned into deserts within the next few years."

For a moment Jessie sat in silence, a thoughtful frown forming on her face. Then she said, "That sounds terribly drastic, Walter. It's lucky that I got here when I did. Tell me what's happening to the farmlands."

"You know that since irrigation has become so popular, the valley farms depend on water from the rivers that flow down from the Sierras to make their crops," Edmonds began.

"Of course," Jessie nodded. "Alex was one of the few who saw the potential for crop irrigation."

"Yes," the banker agreed. "But that was before the day of the large-scale placer mining. Oh, there were a few miners who worked placer claims up in the Mother Lode, but noting compared to what's looming now."

"But even if the placer miners move down from the Mother Lode into the valleys, I still don't see how that's going to harm the farms," Jessie objected. "After all, it would take a lot of miners—thousands of them—panning for gold on rivers as big as the Sacramento and San Joaquin to do the kind of damage you're suggesting."

"I'm not just suggesting it, Jessie. I'm telling you that it's about to happen," Edmonds said soberly. "How long has it been since you've been in placer mining country, Jessie?"

"Why, several years. But I've seen placer mining in a number of places—Montana, the Dakota country, and before that in the Mother Lode."

"Placer mining today doesn't mean what it did even a few years ago," Edmonds told her. "Today, it's not a bunch

32

of individual miners panning in the shallows. Now, placer mining is being done by gold dredges, machines that scoop up soil from the bottom in the shallows along the banks and wash the gold out in big troughs."

"Surely the dredges wouldn't be as bad as hydraulic mining!" Jessie protested. "I know what that can do to ruin cropland. But California's barred the big hydraulic operations. Alex had a large hand in getting that done, just before . . ." Her voice trailed off as the bitter memory of her beloved father's death flashed into her mind.

Edmonds caught Jessie's mood and said nothing, waiting for her to shake off the unhappy memories. After a moment, he went on, "Yes, I worked on that with Alex, if you remember. There won't be any big monitor hoses in the foothills, washing mountain silt into the creeks and rivers and cutting down their flow."

"But I don't see how placer mining, whether it's done by hand or with these new dredges you're talking about, can do the kind of damage you're describing to farmland along the bank of a big river."

"Jessie, until you've seen what happens to a stream that's been worked by a gold dredge, please take my word that I'm not just seeing ghosts that don't exist," Edmonds said.

"I'm sure you are right, Walter. Alex made a good judgment and respected your foresightedness when he put you in charge of this bank, and I've come to respect it, too. But what you've said sounds so terrible that I can't quite bring myself to believe it."

"There are some small dredges operating in the Mother Lode and in the foothills south of the old diggings," Edmonds said. "I think you'd better take the time to go look for yourself, if you can stay here long enough."

"I was planning to leave tomorrow," Jessie said.

"Back to the Circle Star, I suppose?"

"Of course. The busiest time of the year for a cattle ranch is just about to come up."

"Your hands can handle things without you being there, can't they?"

"Oh, certainly. But I like to be around myself."

"Just for your own pleasure?" the banker asked.

Jessie smiled. "If you're suggesting I'm selfish in wanting to be at the Circle Star, I suppose you're right. But until you've ridden in a gather and worked cattle on the back of a good horse, I don't think you'll understand."

"Perhaps not," Edmonds said. "Well, I've given you the best advice I can, Jessie. Whether you take it is up to you."

"I've never had bad advice from you," Jessie told the banker. "And I'm sure what you've said is—well, I'm sure you aren't seeing ghosts under the bed." She stopped, thought for a moment, then went on, "Walter, if the California legislature could pass a law banning large-scale hydraulic mining, couldn't it pass another law banning these dredges you say are so bad?"

"I think perhaps you'd better ask a lawyer about that. I'm just a banker," Edmonds replied.

"I intend to," Jessie said. "In fact, I'd planned to go on to Frank Allison's office after I visited you." She stood up and Edmonds followed suit. "Thanks for telling me about the problem, Walter. I'll let you know my plans after I've talked to Frank. If he agrees with you, or perhaps even if he doesn't, I'll put off going back until I find out how big a fight I'm going to have to make to save the valley farmland."

Chapter 4

As Jessie walked the half block down Montgomery Street to the building that housed the offices of the Starbuck attorneys, she paid little attention to the bustling crowds that now filled the sidewalks. Her mind was preoccupied with the unpleasant vista sketched by Walter Edmonds. She entered the yellow brick building, nodded to a young clerk who greeted her as she came into the lobby, and followed him down the hall to a door which bore the name of the firm's senior member in its frosted glass upper panel.

When the clerk announced Jessie's name Frank Allison rose from his desk, and stepped around it to take her hand. As he walked with her to his desk he said, "I was wondering when you'd be here, Jessie. Our calender clerk gave me a memo yesterday mentioning that you and Ki were on the list of witnesses at a Coast Guard hearing this morning. What sort of trouble did you two get into?"

"We had a brush with some thugs on the ship coming down here from Seattle," Jessie replied. "But the hearing was only a formality. I didn't think I needed to have you there."

"It's over now, I suppose?"

"Finished and closed. I dropped in to sign those new timber leases that you were checking over."

"They're all ready for you, Jessie." Allison tapped the bell on his desk and in a moment the young clerk opened the door and came in. Allison said, "Bring me the Starbuck timber leases, Dennis."

Jessie broke in, "While I'm here, perhaps we'd better have a look at the farmland leases. I stopped at the bank to say hello to Walter Edmonds, and he gave me some disturbing news about the farmers who're leasing Starbuck land in both the San Joaquin and Sacramento valleys."

Allison nodded to the clerk, who started back to the outer office. When the young man had closed the door, the lawyer turned to Jessie and said, "My guess is that Walter's concerned about the dredging threat. Am I right?"

Jessie nodded. "He seems quite upset. I told him I'd ask you about it."

Abruptly, the lawyer changed the subject. He asked Jessie, "Have you ever watched one of the little gold dredges that're in operation now in the Mother Lode country?"

"No. The closest I've ever been to a gold dredge was a few years ago when I was up in Montana, and that was just a glimpse of one from the window of the stagecoach I was traveling in. All I could see was a sort of flat-bottomed boat out in the middle of a lot of rocks."

"That's about as good a description as I could have given you," Allison said. "I just wondered if you know how dredges operate."

"I think so," she said. "They pan for gold on a very large scale, as I understand it. The dredge moves like a boat and has a chain of scoops that scrape up sand and mud and rocks from the river bottom, and a sluice that carries a stream of running water. The scoops dump the soil and rocks into the sluice where the water washes the gold out. Because gold is so heavy, the flakes settle to the bottom of the sluice, and the operator scrapes them up."

When Jessie paused, Allison said, "I couldn't have done any better if I'd been describing a dredge for a legal brief,

36

but you missed a couple of points. The first is that dredges can operate profitably if there's as little as an eighth of an ounce of gold in every ton of river bottom soil they handle, so they can work in streams that a placer miner using a pan couldn't afford to touch."

"And what's the other point I missed?" she asked when the lawyer paused.

"A dredge leaves a tremendous amount of waste, which is all piled up in straight rows behind the dredge, with the rocks on top of the piles, and that's what the farmers are so concerned about."

Jessie nodded. "Yes, that's what bothered the ranchers up in Montana, too. They said that land worked by a dredge won't grow grass or wheat for a hundred years. They tried to get dredging outlawed, but the Montana Supreme Court ruled that the dredges were simply large-scale placer mining."

"I'm familiar with that ruling," Allison nodded. "I had one of our clerks do some research when this first began."

"Then I suppose you know what the situation is here in the California valleys?" she asked.

"I'm just beginning to investigate it," the attorney told her. "We have some other clients who're in the same position you are, Jessie. Like you, they own substantial acreage in the Sacramento and San Joaquin valleys and they're quite upset about the prospect of these new, big gold dredges they've heard about operating in the rivers. I've been doing a little research to see what can be done."

"What have you found out?"

"That there's plenty of reason for them to be worried. But right now, I'm not sure—" He broke off as the clerk tapped lightly on the door and came in carrying two bulging Manila file folders. He put them on Allison's desk and left. The attorney went on, "I'm not sure there's any immediate

37

threat to the lower valleys where most of the Starbuck land is located, but I can see trouble beginning very soon on the tributaries."

"Won't it just be a matter of time before the dredges move downstream, though?" Jessie frowned.

"That's a question I can't answer yet, Jessie," Allison confessed. "So far, all we have to go on is rumors. Nobody's been able to get a good look at the new dredges or even find out who's building them."

"Wouldn't the law against hydraulic mining that you and Alex got the legislature to pass stop gold dredging as well?"

Allison shook his head. "There's quite a difference. I don't know how much you recall about the details of the fight Alex got involved in trying to stop the big hydraulic mining stands, but the two situations aren't the same."

"Alex told me a little bit about what he was doing, but all I remember is that he said it would protect all the farmers who got irrigation water from the rivers," Jessie said. "That was a long time ago, Frank. I was still going to school. I didn't see Alex very often while I was at Miss Booth's Academy—just when I'd go to the Circle Star during vacation, or when he'd stop to visit me during one of his trips East."

"Well, his fight against the monitors washing away the land got the California legislature to join the other western states and put the rivers under the U.S. government's water use laws. That's why we're looking at the beginning of another fight."

"Maybe you'd better explain from the beginning," Jessie suggested. "Where does the federal government come in?"

"Oh, that goes back a long way, but I'll make it as short a story as I can." Allison settled back into his chair and went on, "The federal government stepped in when settlers began moving West and steamboats started navigating the rivers. The states passed so many conflicting laws covering

38

riverboats that the U.S. government took over jurisdiction of the streams."

"But what does that have to do with the gold dredges?" Jessie asked.

"There's a very direct connection," the lawyer told her. "Hydraulic gold mining ruined a lot of the Mother Lode country by blocking creeks and small rivers with mud and silt. At that time there wasn't any California law that gave the farmers downstream a right to water. The new United States law gives some rights to farmers and gristmills and other water users downstream, but it also preserves the rights of the small placer miners to pan for gold upstream."

"How?" Jessie asked when Allison paused for breath.

"One section of the U.S. water rights law is called the 'arid region right,'" the lawyer went on. "Congress intended it to protect the downstream water users, farmers and ranchers, without stopping placer mining in the headwaters of a creek or river. I won't bother you with all the details, but any placer miner who owns the land he's working or has a mining claim on it can use all the water he needs."

"By 'all,' do you mean a hundred percent?" Jessie asked. When Allison nodded, she went on, "How does that protect the ranchers and farmers downstream, then?"

Allison smiled. "The law has another clause. Before a placer miner can shut off a stream completely, he's required to notify all downstream water users and get their consent."

"Then, if even a single farmer can stop the placer miners from completely cutting off the flow of a creek or river, why are they so afraid of the gold dredges?"

"Most laws are based on theory, Jessie," Allison replied. "And a lot of them that are good in theory have loopholes that defeat their own purpose."

"What's the loophole in this 'arid region right,' then?"

"It gives the operators of gold dredges the rights that were originally intended to protect individual placer miners who'd filed on a small claim up at the headwaters of a river or some of its tributaries," Allison replied.

"To use all the water they want to, unless some farmer with land downstream objects?"

Allison nodded, then went on, "The loophole is that the gold dredges work in the shallow water along the riverbanks. From what I've been able to dig up so far, the catch is that these big new dredges won't stop the rivers from flowing, but they'll pile up an unbroken line of debris in the shallows that will simply cut off the farmers's fields from the water."

"Why, that would make irrigated farming impossible!" Jessie protested.

"Of course, it would," Allison agreed. "The farmers along the rivers have their own name for the dredge operators; they're calling them 'placer pirates.'"

"What's going to happen when the farmers can't get a flow of irrigation water through the debris the dredges have left?"

"They say they'll fight, right to the point of dynamiting the dredges, and I believe them, Jessie. I'll go even further and tell you I don't blame them."

"Frank, have you been able to find out who's building these new dredges?" Jessie inquired.

"Not so far, and it hasn't been for lack of trying."

"Then you don't know whether they're big, well-financed companies, or just a few miners who've struck it rich and see a chance to get even richer?"

"I do know there haven't been any large new companies formed to operate dredges or do placer mining," the attorney answered. "But there's no law that stops an existing company from expanding by adding another kind of business to its charter."

For a long moment Jessie was silent; then she said slowly, "I suppose you've guessed what I'm getting at."

"I think so. Alex's old enemy. Your enemy, now."

"Yes. The cartel."

For a moment the lawyer said nothing; then he told Jessie, "You know the situation I'm in where your fight with the cartel's concerned. You can't go by the rule book when you fight it, and if I know in advance you may do something illegal, I'm as guilty as you are. In effect, I become your accomplice and face disbarment. We'd better not talk about the cartel, Jessie."

"We don't need to, Frank," Jessie said. "You've told me what I need to know." She indicated the two piles of papers on the attorney's desk and went on, "I'll sign those timberland leases now, and I won't need to go over the others."

"They're here whenever you need them, of course," Allison said as he pushed the timberland leases across the desk and gave Jessie a pen.

"I may later," Jessie told him as she began signing. "But I've decided to change my plans. Much as I'd like to go back to the Circle Star, I won't be leaving for Texas right away. Ki and I are going to take a little trip first. It's been a long time since I've been up to the Mother Lode country."

"Of course, Nate Wheeler might not even be in Rough and Ready any longer," Ki reminded Jessie as they reined in to rest their horses at the top of an especially steep section of the trail. "You got that letter from him almost six months ago."

"Yes, I know," she nodded. "But if you remember, he wrote in the letter that he was trying to scrape together enough money to buy a piece of land with a cabin on it near the town because he was getting too old to keep traveling around trying to make a good strike."

"All prospectors have itchy feet, Jessie," Ki said. "But I suppose we've got to start somewhere, and I agree with you that Nate's our best bet."

After Jessie's conversations with Edmonds and Allison,

she'd wasted no time. She and Ki had left for the Mother Lode the day after her visits to the bank and the lawyer's office. They had a short, comfortable first-day trip on the new Central Pacific line from Oakland to Auburn and changed there to one of the surviving short-haul railroads built in the flush of the big gold strikes to run to San Francisco Bay from the Grass Valley and Nevada City workings.

Out of Auburn, they suffered through a day's travel in a creaking passenger coach drawn by an asthmatic loco-motive to Grass Valley, where they rented livery stable horses to make the last leg of their journey to visit Alex's old friend, Nate Wheeler.

From the crest where they'd stopped to breathe their mounts, the spine of the Sierra Nevada cut the skyline to their right, the land sloping up obliquely to rugged peaks. Ahead, dark streaks marked the course of countless creeks and brooks that ran down between the ridges of the long western Sierra slope. On all sides the marks of the sudden invasion of the forty-niners and their thousands of successors were still visible.

Several hundred yards up the slope from where Jessie and Ki sat on their horses, a small creek meandered in sinuous curves. They could see the water's surface only in places where the broken ground dipped along the stream's banks to show the sun's rays dancing on blue water. The creek trickled down the long slant to the Sacramento river valley, and the valley lost itself in the distant haze which began to blur the clear air near the base of the foothills.

Where the pine forest had once covered the slopes there were now saplings growing between aging stumps of trees that had been cut hastily to provide the lumber for sluices, cabins, and the firewood that was so necessary during the long mile-high winters. In a few places even the stumps had been cut to ground-level, and in several of these cleared spots there were jumbled piles of weathered logs, all that remained of cabins abandoned when a placer claim had been worked out.

As Jessie scanned the landscape ahead, she saw in the distance beyond the creek an immense expanse of raw brown soil stretching away from the base of a bluff, and that soil somehow seemed out of place in the rolling foothill country. She pointed it out to Ki, and said, "That can't be cultivated ground, Ki. We're too high now to run into a farm."

"No, it's not a farm," Ki told her. "That's where a monitor was operated at one time, before hydraulic gold mining was stopped."

"You know, Alex told me about the monitors, and I got a quick glimpse of one from the window of a train when he took me to California for a vacation one year. But this is the first chance I've had to get close enough to see what they did. It's not too far out of our way, Ki. Let's take a closer look at the place. I'm curious."

They toed their horses into motion, heading now for the bare bluff that loomed ahead. As they drew closer, the devastation wrought by the six-inch stream of water shot from the nozzle of the now outlawed monitor became increasingly visible. The huge water-jet had sliced into the side of what had been an unusually large hill and washed it away in a wide shallow arc. A few of the big timbers that had supported the sluice were still standing at one side of the cut, rising starkly white from the brown soil.

When they reached the first of these timbers, Ki reined in and pointed down the slope, where the dry bed of a creek emerged from the edge of the barren area. In its center a widely spaced row of blocks made from large, squared stones ran down the gentle incline to the creek bed.

"Those timbers are where the sluice ran," he said. "They probably built a dam across the creek up above somewhere; it'd have to be quite a bit higher than the monitor nozzle to give them enough pressure to shoot that six-inch stream

43

of water to the face of the hill. Those blocks of stone were set to anchor the monitor when it had to be moved up at different times."

"They moved it forward as the water ate away the bluff, then?" Jessie asked.

Ki replied, "I'd guess that the nearest of them is where the monitor stood when hydraulic mining was shut down."

"I wondered why they left part of the hill standing," she said. "But that makes sense. I suppose the monitor had some value as salvage, so they just took it off and left the foundations because it was too much trouble to move them."

"More than likely," Ki agreed.

Jessie was looking at the barren ground on the slope that led away from the sheer face of what remained of the hill. "If a gold dredge does more damage to the land than this kind of mining did, I'm ready to do almost anything within reason to stop the dredges, Ki. It's going to take years before this bare soil is fertile enough to grow grass or trees or anything else again."

"I don't know much about dredges, Jessie," Ki said. "I remember what the ranchers up in Montana told us a couple of years ago, and I'll certainly agree with you."

"I've seen enough," Jessie said. "Let's move along. If the country ahead's not any worse than what we've been traveling over, we ought to get to Rough and Ready before dark."

They rode on along the winding trail through the new pine growth while the sunny afternoon waned. From the trail they saw two ghost towns in the distance. Tumbledown houses marked the end of dreams of sudden wealth for some of the forty-niners. What they'd taken for a rich lode petered out. The bottom of the sun was just disappearing in the haze that still shrouded the western horizon when they saw a cluster of cabins and houses around a number of larger

44

structures that they identified as stores when they drew closer.

"That's got to be Rough and Ready," Jessie said. "I'm sure we can ask where Nate's cabin is at one of the stores."

Within the following quarter hour they could see that the town was much larger than it had appeared from the trail. The houses that had looked aimlessly sprawling were on narrow, short dirt streets which crossed the wider main street that formed the town's center. At close range, they looked a bit better than they had from a distance. Almost half of them were painted and all but a few of them had glass windows through which curtains were visible. Along the main street there were a dozen well-kept stores and a half-dozen saloons. A few buggies and a number of horses stood at hitchrails in front of the structures, and there were pedestrians on the board sidewalks.

At the livery stable, Ki went in to buy grain for the horses and to get exact directions to Nate's cabin. When he came out he nodded to Jessie as he swung into his saddle and said, "They knew Nate, all right. His cabin is off to the northeast, about a mile and a half from town. There's only one trail, so we can't miss it."

They rode on beyond the town, and once again found themselves on a trail that wound through a stand of second-growth pines, which grew between the stumps of older trees. The trail was shaded now in the approaching dusk.

After they'd ridden a quarter of an hour, Jessie said, "If Nate's cabin is only a mile and a half from town, we ought to see it pretty soon."

"Yes, it can't be too far—" Ki began. He stopped short as a rifle shot rang through the trees ahead, followed by a second shot.

"I think we got here just in time," Jessie said, pulling her rifle from its saddle scabbard. "Unless there's another cabin on this trail, those shots came from Nate's, and that means he's in trouble. Come on, Ki! He might need our help!"

Chapter 5

Another shot sounded ahead before Jessie and Ki rounded the next bend in the winding path. Now they could see that the trail widened to create a small clearing in the dense second-growth that elsewhere was almost impenetrably thick on both sides of the path. As they drew closer they saw the corner of a log cabin, set cater-cornered to the trail, giving them a glimpse of the windows that broke the cabin's end and side walls.

Suddenly the barrel of a rifle was thrust from the end window. They saw a streak of red muzzle-blast spurt from the rifle and a split-second later the crack of the shot reached their ears. From the thicket of small bushy pines that covered the ground beyond the cabin in such profusion that in places their lower branches entwined, another rifle cracked. Now, Jessie and Ki were close enough to hear the bullet thunk into the cabin's sturdy log wall.

Jessie had not seen the muzzle-blast of the rifle fired from the pine thicket. She scanned the wall of trees, and even though she found no clue to the location of the shooter, she let off an answering shot into the brush. At almost the same time the cabin's defender fired again and at once a third shot broke the air from the side of the trail fifty yards ahead of them.

"I spotted where that second shot came from," Ki said. He slid out of his saddle and dropped the reins over his

47

horse's head. "You take cover, Jessie. I'll slip into the brush here and circle around. Maybe I can come up behind whoever fired it."

Jessie turned her mount on the trail and leaned from her saddle to grab the reins Ki had dropped before he disappeared into the brush. Leading the second horse, she toed her own steed into the concealing growth on the opposite side of the trail.

Two more shots shattered the still air, one from the cabin, the second from the forest beyond it, before she could tether the horses and start circling the little clearing in which the cabin stood. She stopped, waiting for another shot to pinpoint a target. A half minute ticked off, then another, but both the cabin and the small pines surrounding remained quiet.

Jessie was now on the side of the cabin opposite the path, some distance from the spot where Ki had left the trail, and the next shot from the brush sounded fainter than the one that she'd heard ahead of her. The rifle barrel that had been pushing from the end window suddenly disappeared, and in a moment Jessie heard its bark from the side of the cabin that she could not see. The gunman, hidden in the brush ahead of her, fired at once.

Though Jessie had only heard the shot, she swung her rifle to cover the area from which it had come and quickly triggered off another round. Before the echoes of her gun's report had died away, a man's voice coming from the dense growth in front of her reached Jessie's ears.

"Get the hell outta here, Blackie!" he shouted. "We got ourselves whipsawed!"

Jessie fired again in the direction from which the voice had sounded, but a rustling of disturbed foliage followed by the thudding of hoofbeats told her that the man who'd been shooting from that side was making his getaway. Then the hoofbeats of a more distant horse thumped briefly and faded, and she guessed that Ki had missed finding his quarry as well.

For a moment or two Jessie stood listening as the hoof-beats and whipping of disturbed low-growing branches subsided, and when the forest and cabin were both silent she turned and walked back to where she'd left the horses. Picking up their reins, she led them to where she could see the trail again. She did not leave the concealing brush, but kept in the cover of the pines as she started toward the cabin. Reaching the edge of the little clearing in which it stood, she stopped.

"Nate!" Jessie called. "Nate Wheeler! Don't shoot! This is Jessie Starbuck! It's safe for you to come out, now. The men who were shooting at you have gone!"

There was no immediate reply from the cabin, but Jessie saw the door open an inch or two. Then it opened wide and a man came out. In the years that had passed since Jessie had last seen Nate, age had changed him, but even in the blue dusk that warned of the quick approach of darkness she recognized him.

"Jessie!" Nate exclaimed.

He started forward along the path and Jessie stepped out of the brush. She took the gnarled horn-hard hand Nate extended and held it in both of hers while they looked at one another. She could see more clearly the changes time had wrought in the old prospector since she'd last seen him a number of years ago. Nate's short trimmed beard was almost pure white and the deep brown tan she remembered had paled. His sturdy shoulders sagged and his entire body seemed to have diminished in size.

Nate said, "Dog me if it ain't you in the flesh, Jessie! What in tucket are you doing way out here in Californiy?"

"I had some business in San Francisco," Jessie replied.

"Then I found that I needed to talk to you, so here I am."

"And you came all the way up here to the Mother Lode to find me?" Nate asked.

"Of course," Jessie smiled. "Ki's with me; he'll be along in a minute or so."

"Well, I tell you, you're welcome as the flowers in May," Nate said. "I couldn't figure out who it was shooting at them fellers that had me holed up, but I was sure glad to hear 'em say they was taking off."

"Who were they, Nate?" Jessie asked. "And why were they shooting at you?"

Nate was silent for a moment, then he said, "That's a sorta long story. If you ain't in a right big hurry, I'll put off telling you till we get inside the cabin and I light a lamp so I can fix up my arm."

For the first time Jessie saw that the left sleeve of the old miner's blue denim shirt was stained with blood. "Why didn't you tell me you'd been hit?" she asked.

"Shucks, it ain't only a scratch, Jessie. If I'd of been watching my p's and q's, I'd've heard them blacklegs while they was sneaking up to my cabin. But I was over on the other side of the clearing chopping wood when they cut loose, and one of 'em winged me before I could dive in the door."

Restraining her curiosity, Jessie followed Nate into the cabin. Even in the dim interior light she could see that it was little different from dozens of others that she'd seen at similar places during her travels.

Dominating the windowless end of the single rectangular room was a fireplace of rough-hewn stone. Two windows had been cut in the back wall; another opened at Jessie's right, a few feet from the door; a fourth was centered in the end wall opposite the fireplace. None of the windows had glass panes; they were closed by shutters. The shutters of the two windows from which Nate had been firing at his attackers were ajar, allowing a bit of the fading daylight to trickle in.

A spartan simplicity was reflected in the cabin's interior. A tanned bearskin covered most of the packed earth floor. A pair of bunkbeds were in the corner. A table of rough-hewn lumber stood in the center of the room, two chairs pulled up to it; a third chair stood against the end wall. Shelves on both sides of the fireplace filled the windowless wall; they held a few unidentifiable bags and packages as well as some tin plates and cups. A spider, a deep iron skillet, and stew pot stood on the hearth.

An unlighted lantern hung from the hooked end of a stout wire fastened to the ceiling in the room's center, and Nate lifted it off and set it on the table.

"There's some matches on the hearth, Jessie," Nate said. "If you'll kindly light the lantern, I'll shutter up the windows."

"Hadn't we better bandage your arm first?" she asked.

"It ain't hurting me all that bad," Nate replied, starting toward the window in the back wall. "Besides, them fellows that was shooting at me might not stay scared, and I'd rather shut up these windows before we do anything more."

Jessie carried the lantern to the hearth and was just touching one of the sputtering matches to its wick when Ki called from outside, "Jessie? Are you all right?"

"I'm fine, Ki," she replied. Dropping the lantern's glass chimney, she went on, "Come on in. We'll tend to the horses and bring our gear in later, after I've bandaged Nate's arm."

"Is he hurt badly?" Ki asked as he entered.

Nate stepped away from the window he was latching and said, "All I got is a little scratch, Ki. But it's right fine to see you again. Sorta reminds me of old times when—" Suddenly aware that the mention of Alex Starbuck's name might stir unhappy memories for Jessie, he stopped abruptly. Pausing long enough to exchange a handclasp with Ki, he

51

moved on to the last window and latched it, saying over his shoulder to Jessie, "Might be it's a good idea to bring your gear inside. The horses oughta be all right if you tether 'em close by the door."

"I'll take care of them," Ki volunteered. He indicated the bloodstain on Nate's shirtsleeve and said to Jessie, "You can fix Nate up while I'm getting our gear inside."

"I got a little pot of bear grease on one of them shelves by the chimney," Nate said, obeying Jessie's gesture by settling into a chair beside the table. As he began rolling up his sleeve he went on, "It'll heal me up quicker'n any of them new-fangled salves doctors smears on a man nowadays."

A quick glance told Jessie that Nate had been right when he described the bullet wound as a scratch. The slug had cut a raw shallow crease at the base of his biceps above the elbow. Though the skin around the crease was still an angry red, the wound had already formed a thin scab and was no longer bleeding. Bear grease, Jessie decided, was as good a salve as any other.

"I'll need a strip of cloth to bandage your arm with," she told Nate, looking around the bare little cabin.

"Well, there's an old shirt I started tearing up awhile back," he said. "It's on that upper bunk. I'll just drag it out for you, Jessie."

"Never mind, I'll find it," Jessie replied.

She found both the pot of bear grease and the remains of the tattered denim shirt and was just tying off the bandage she'd made from a strip of the denim when Ki returned carrying their saddlebags.

"Everything's quiet outside," he reported. "It's not very likely that those men who were shooting at you will be back, Nate. Who were they? And why were they trying to kill you?"

Nate began rolling his shirtsleeve down and kept his head

52

averted until he'd buttoned the cuff. At last he sighed and shook his head as he lifted it to face Jessie and Ki.

"I guess I better lay it all out on the level," he said. "I know Alex never had no use for liars, Jessie, and I figure you to be pretty much like him."

"If we're going to help you, we've got to know the facts," Jessie replied. "Whatever trouble you're in, Ki and I will do our best to get it straightened out."

"Of course, we will!" Ki seconded, sitting down across the table from Nate and Jessie.

"Well, I take that kindly, Ki. And you, too, Jessie," the old miner said. "And I oughta've had more sense than to get myself into a squeeze like I did. But I'm in it, and there ain't no use in beating around the bush with you."

"Go on, then," Jessie nodded.

"There was two things got it all started," Nate began. "I taken that money you sent me, Jessie, and put it with what little bit I had, and bought me this cabin. And I aim to pay you back soon as I can."

"No, Nate," Jessie said quickly. "I know you did a lot of things for Alex when he was just beginning to get started, and I'm sure at that time he couldn't afford to pay you what you were worth to him. Think of the money I sent you as back pay."

"Your pa never owed me nor nobody else a dime that he didn't pay up when it was due," Nate told Jessie. "So I figure I owe you what you sent me, and—"

"Let's talk about that later," Jessie broke in. "Right now I'm interested in finding the reason those two men were shooting at you."

"Sure," Nate nodded. He went on, "Like I started to say, after I got me this cabin free and clear, I rested a little while; then I begun doing some prospecting again. Maybe my luck was just in, or maybe I know more'n I used to, but whichever it was, before too long, I run into some of the purtiest color

53

you ever seen. That was on the middle fork of the Yuba, up above French Corral. My panning was so rich I figured that after all these years I might've stumbled onto the real Mother Lode."

"Nate, you've been prospecting long enough to know by now that there's no such thing as a Mother Lode," Ki broke in when the old man paused. "That big gold deposit the oldtimers thought was the source of all the gold in the Sierra foothills just doesn't exist."

"Well, now, Ki, maybe it don't and maybe it does," Nate shot back. "But regardless, that strike up on the Yuba was the best one I ever hit, and I taken a lot of gold outta it." He turned back to Jessie and went on, "Not just dust, neither. I had me two bags of nuggets bigger'n my thumb in less'n a month of panning, and seven bags of fine gold. Only by then I was close to running outta grub, so I figured I'd come back here, rest a week or so, send you the money I owed you, buy what I was needing, and then go back and pan some more. And that was when I made my mistake."

Jessie and Ki waited when the old miner shook his head and fell silent. At last Jessie said, "Go on. Finish telling us."

"It ain't easy to talk about, Jessie," Nate replied. "And I ain't sure it'd be proper to go on with a young lady like you listening to me."

"I'm a grown-up woman now, Nate," Jessie told him. "Not the little girl I was when you saw me last. There's very little I haven't seen or heard about, so you can't shock or embarrass me easily."

"Reckon you are, at that," he agreed.

"Finish your story, then," she suggested.

"Well, it might be you've guessed what I don't like to talk about," Nate went on, dropping his head forward as though he was speaking to the top of the table. "But I done what the good book says not to. I looked on the wine when it was red and I taken up with scarlet women and gamblers."

Aware that with his head averted Nate could not see her, Jessie signaled with her eyes to Ki that she wanted him to take up the questioning. She was sure that the old prospector would respond to Ki more readily than to a woman.

Ki waited a moment before saying, "It's not an uncommon thing to happen, Nate. You're not the only man who's been caught by whores and gamblers. I suppose you spent all your money and then ran up a big debt in the games?"

"That's about the size of it, Ki," Nate agreed. "I guess you're right. I seen fellers do what I done, but I always figured I'd be too smart to play the fool that way."

"Then those two men who were shooting at you had come to collect your gambling debts?" Ki went on.

"Yep," Nate nodded. "But I ain't told you the worst of it yet. You see, part of the time I was drunk enough to brag about that rich new claim I'd found, so them gamblers told me they'd give me credit. Course, I went on playing, but all I done was run up a bigger tab. I figured they'd wait till I could go back to my dig and pan out however much gold I needed to pay 'em, but they said that wasn't good enough."

"So they told you that you'd have to sign your claim over to them?" Ki asked when Nate fell silent again.

"You hit it square on the head," Nate replied. "But I'd sobered up enough by then so I seen that wasn't the right thing for me to do. I said no, and right then they pulled out their guns and told me I'd do it or else."

"Or else they'd kill you?" Ki suggested, and again Nate nodded.

Jessie judged that with his story started it was safe for her to interpose a question. She asked the old man, "Where did all this happen?"

"Why, in Rough and Ready, Jessie. You'd've had to come through there on your way, but I don't guess you taken a good look at the town. It might not look like much, but it's got some pretty big-time gamblers there. After they closed down the big hydraulic monitors, this part of the Mother Lode's about the only place left where there's a lot of claims still producing and a lot of prospecting done."

"I'll admit the town didn't impress me," she said. "But you'd certainly know about it."

Again, Nate nodded. Then, his voice doleful, he went on, "I still ain't finished telling you what all happened."

"Go on, then," Ki said.

"Well, when them gamblers stuck their guns in my belly, one on each side of me, I told 'em my claim proof was out here at the cabin. I don't know as you'd understand about that, but nowadays when you file a claim you got to go to the county seat to register it, and the clerk gives you a proof certificate. It's sorta like the title papers I got when I bought my place here."

"And you didn't deliver the certificate to them?" Ki asked when Nate paused again.

"Worse'n that, Ki. I was sobered up pretty good after all that had happened, and when one of them fellers started out here with me to get the certificate, I watched for my chance and jumped him. We had a hell of a fight, if you'll excuse my language, Jessie. After all the work I done, I'm stronger'n I look, and he wasn't being real careful about keeping an eye on me. Anyways, I just beat him till he couldn't fight no more and left him on the trail."

"When did all this happen?" Jessie asked.

"Four days ago."

"And they didn't come out until today?"

Nate shook his head. "Them two men that jumped me wasn't the gamblers themselves, Jessie. I know everybody that hangs out in the saloons and gambling houses in Rough and Ready. Them fellers was hired from someplace else. I got a real good look at 'em before they told me what they was after, and I never had seen 'em in town."

56

"That would mean they'd have to be connected with crooks in another town," Jessie frowned. "Not exactly what I'd expect from gamblers operating in a small place like Rough and Ready."

"They ain't small-timers," Nate said earnestly. "There's a lot of gold dust and nuggets changes hands in them games they run. And they own the saloon, too, and the—the—"

Jessie finished for him, "The whorehouse?"

Nate nodded silently.

"They sound pretty well organized," Ki observed.

"Yes," Jessie nodded. "Very well, indeed. And bringing in hired gunmen from outside town gives me an idea that the gamblers Nate's in trouble with just might be part of a much larger organization than appears on the surface."

"You have the same thought I do," Ki said quietly.

"It would fit the pattern that Frank Allison mentioned in passing when we were talking in San Francisco, too," Jessie went on. "From what Nate's told us, there's a lot more wealth here in this part of the Mother Lode than there ever was before. And wherever there's wealth, the leeches show up sooner or later. The kind of organization Nate's described means just one thing that I can see, Ki."

"Yes," Ki said soberly. "The cartel."

Chapter 6

"Hold on, Ki," Nate said. "Seems like you and Jessie led me out to where the water's over my boot-tops. This cartel you're talking about, is it a what or a who?"

Jessie and Ki exchanged glances; after so many years of working together, they needed no words to agree that Nate should be taken at least partly into their confidence. When Jessie nodded, Ki turned back to Nate.

"Let's just call the cartel a gang, Nate," he suggested. "A big gang that might run some legitimate businesses as a cover, but underneath is really a bunch of cutthroats."

Nate nodded slowly, then said, "That'd mean it's something like the Sydney Ducks and them other crooked outfits that used to run the Barbary Coast in San Francisco back in the old days when I first come out here, I guess."

"Something like that," Jessie replied. "Except it's a much bigger gang than the ones you're thinking of, and a lot worse than I've ever heard the Sydney Ducks and those others were."

A thoughtful frown had grown on Nate's grizzled face. He said, "You know, Jessie, it might be a gang, at that. I never gave it much thought before, but Rough and Ready's sure changed a lot since I first came here, and most of them changes has been what most folks don't call respectable."

"Maybe you'd better explain what you mean, Nate," Jessie suggested.

"Well, when I got here, Rough and Ready didn't have but one little run-down gambling house and two saloons, and if you'll excuse my plain language, Jessie, there were maybe six or eight girls down in the red light district. But all of a sudden three big new gambling places and four more saloons and a parlor house opened up and pretty soon the town got to be the way it is now."

"This happened very quickly, then?" Ki asked.

"Less'n a year, give or take," Nate replied. "Course, I wasn't in town all the time, Ki. I was prospecting along the forks of the Yuba River and a lot of little creeks higher up in the foothills."

"But the change must have been very fast, or you wouldn't have given it much thought," Jessie said.

"I guess you could put it that way," Nate agreed. "It sorta reminded me of when the Gold Rush begun back in forty-nine, only I know dang good and well there ain't that many new prospectors coming up to the Mother Lode right now, and I couldn't see much reason for all them new places."

"Do all of them seem to be making money?" Jessie asked.

"I reckon they are, Jessie," Nate replied. "Even if there ain't a big lot of new prospectors coming in, them new dredges the damn placer pirates is building is drawing a lot of Chinks up here to do the coolie labor."

Jessie stared at Nate, a frown growing on her face. She asked him, "Somebody's building new gold dredges in Rough and Ready?"

"Oh, they ain't building 'em right in town," Nate replied. "But from what I hear, them damn placer outfits is building five or six real big ones."

"If they're not building the dredges in Rough and Ready, Nate, where are they working?" Ki asked.

"Well, now I don't rightly know where all of 'em is being put together, Ki. All I know about is the two they was getting ready to go to work on alongside some of them creeks that feeds the middle fork of the Yuba."

"But you've heard of others?" Jessie pressed. When Nate nodded, she asked, "When did you see those two you mentioned?"

"I stumbled onto where they was working on 'em one day when I was out prospecting. It was just a little while before I made the big strike I told you about."

"That would have been soon after you bought this cabin, then?" Ki asked.

"Right soon," Nate nodded. "Like I told you a while ago, I ain't been doing a lot of panning since then, so I never did get back to the place where they was working."

"Are you sure they were gold dredges?" Jessie asked.

Nate replied a bit indignantly, "Course, I'm sure, Jessie! I seen enough dredges around the diggin' down in the Mariposa country to know what I'm lookin' at, even if these is going to be a lot bigger. Course, I didn't git to look long. There was a couple of uglies with rifles started towards me, and I skedaddled."

"Armed guards?" Jessie frowned.

"If they wasn't, they sure looked like it," Nate nodded.

Ki broke into the conversation between Jessie and Nate to ask her, "Doesn't that fit in with what Frank Allison and Walter Edmonds told you in San Francisco?"

"It does seem to be part of the same pattern, Ki," Jessie agreed. "But all they've had to go on is rumors and gossip that trickled down to San Francisco from up here in the Mother Lode. I'd say Nate knows more than they did."

"I'm sure he does," Ki nodded. Then he turned to Nate and asked, "Didn't you say there were a lot of Chinese working on the two dredges you saw up on the Yuba?"

"Yep," Nate nodded. "Maybe twenty men was on the job, all told, and more'n half of 'em was Chinks."

Ki went on, "Have you seen more Chinese than usual in

Rough and Ready since you ran into the dredge construction job?"

Nate scratched his grizzled chin before replying; then he said, "Maybe I have, Ki, but I can't rightly say. There's always been a lot of 'em around here, but I can't tell you how many. I just don't go meddling around in Chinatown."

"You mean that Rough and Ready has a Chinese settlement?" Jessie asked. "It's funny that Ki and I didn't notice it when we passed through town."

"It ain't likely you would have, Jessie," Nate told her. "It's a little bit more'n a half mile north of the town."

"How big is it?" Ki asked.

"I ain't paid all that much mind to it, Ki," Nate replied. "Just sorta looked at it while I was passing by. But I'd guess there's maybe fifty or sixty houses and shacks out there."

Turning to Jessie, Ki asked, "You know what I'm thinking?"

"Yes," she nodded. "But I'm not sure it's a good idea, Ki. From what Nate's told us, it's quite a distance from here to where he saw those dredges being built."

"Well, it ain't rightly all that far," the old prospector put in. "Maybe five miles up to French Corral; that's on the south fork of the Yuba. Then it's only about two more miles to the middle fork."

"They were building the dredges right out in the open, where the trail crossed the river, then?" Jessie asked, trying to reconcile an unconcealed construction site with the remark Frank Allison had made about the dredges being built in secrecy.

Nate replied, "Not right along the trail, Jessie. A mile or so way from it, upstream on the creek. If it hadn't been that I was prospecting, I don't guess I'd've stumbled onto 'em. And I didn't waste no time hanging around. Soon as I seen how bad their work was muddying up the creek, I

61

knowed it wouldn't be worth panning, so I turned around and went the other way."

"Seven miles isn't very far to go," Ki frowned. "Jessie, I think it might be a good idea if I went looking for work on that dredge construction job."

Jessie sat for a moment in silent thought, then asked Ki, "What could you find out that would help us?"

"Maybe nothing," Ki shrugged. "Maybe something that would help us. You know I can speak enough Chinese to get by."

"Yes, but what would the laborers know, Ki? They're just hired hands. They wouldn't know who they're really working for."

"I'd be watching as well as working," Ki pointed out.

"Of course," Jessie agreed. "And if you find out anything at all, it will be more than we know now. But—" She turned to Nate and asked, "Did you see a bunkhouse or a cookhouse at the construction job?"

Nate shook his head. "Just a toolshed and a couple of tents was all."

"That would mean the Chinese workers must live here in Rough and Ready, and go home every night," Jessie went on. She asked Ki, "Don't you think it'd be a good idea if we started by taking a look around Rough and Ready first?"

After a moment's thought, Ki nodded. "Yes. I'm sure it would, if only to find out if the dredges really are being built by workers who come back to Rough and Ready every evening." He turned to Nate and asked, "I don't suppose there's anywhere else they could be living, is there?"

"Not a place," Nate replied. "French Corral is closer to it than Rough and Ready, but you couldn't rightly call it a town anymore. It started out to be a pretty good town, but after the diggings there petered out it just about dried up and blowed away. Rough and Ready's the only place near enough for them Chinese to go home to every night."

Nate's tone was so positive that Ki accepted his reply without further probing. He went on, "Are there any gambling houses in the Chinese settlement here?"

"Now, that's something I can't answer," Nate told him. "I never have nosed around the place, Ki. All I know about it is what I heard and what I seen of it from the trail."

Turning back to Jessie, Ki said, "There's only one way to find out what we need to know. I'll have to go take a look."

"I suppose you're right," she agreed. "Tomorrow you can—"

Ki broke in, "Why wait, Jessie? It won't be full dark for another hour, and the trail to town is easy to follow. You can stay here and get settled in while I'm gone."

"It's been a long day," she protested. "Hadn't you better wait? Rest tonight and go look the settlement over tomorrow?"

"Night's the time when the men are there," Ki said. "And if there are any gambling houses, they'd be closed during the daytime. Why put it off, Jessie? The quicker we find out, the better able we'll be to plan our next move."

"If you want me to go along—" Nate volunteered.

Ki shook his head. "No, Nate. I can blend into the settlement; you'd be an outsider. I can't pass for Chinese, but at least I'm an Oriental and can talk their language."

"Ki's right, Nate," Jessie agreed. "We'll stay here, and you can tell me more about those dredges while we're waiting for him to get back."

Though it was the dark of the moon, the night was clear and the stars alone gave enough light to allow Ki to follow the trail from Rough and Ready to the Chinese settlement without trouble. Darkness had fallen when he started from the town, though he'd stopped there only long enough to leave his horse in care of a livery stable and change several double eagles into silver dollars and half dollars. Then he'd started on foot along the well-beaten path to which the liveryman had directed him.

Most of his walk so far had been uphill, but now as the trail descended into a wide shallow valley Ki saw lights glimmering ahead. He moved on without breaking stride as he approached the patch of light slivers, but he began peering carefully at them, trying to determine the lay of the land surrounding the Chinese settlement.

Like so much of the Mother Lode's terrain, the area had been denuded of large trees by the forty-niners. The virgin prospectors had virtually wiped out the original undergrowth as well as the pines of the foothill forests when they'd swarmed into what they'd dreamed of as a promised land where gold nuggets lined the bed of every creek. Although a bit more than thirty years had passed since the first ones arrived, the semiarid foothills of the Mother Lode had been slow to recover.

Except where low bushy digger pines had sprung up, the downslope ahead was barren. With no vegetation to block his vision, Ki had little trouble in identifying the structures that nestled compactly at the bottom of the saucerlike valley. As far as he could make out from the light pattern, the Chinese settlement had simply grown up willy-nilly, not laid out in neat square streets.

Houses crowded together in a mad jumble with only narrow paths between them. Most of the dwellings were small, and many of these were dark. In the center of the settlement there were several larger buildings, two and three stories. Most were dark now, but lights glowed through the windows of the top floor of one, and two of the taller ones were lighted on all three floors. It was toward these that Ki directed his steps.

He passed through the fringe of the fringe of the settlement, a few scattered houses, and began winding through the zigzag passages, alleys rather than streets. As he neared the center of the settlement, Ki became aware that he was no longer alone. Other men, singly and in groups of two, three or four, were also heading for the lighted buildings. Within a few minutes he became part of a crowd. In the darkness that shrouded the narrow lanes, none of the others paid any attention to him.

Ki slowed down just enough to stay with the others, and he was soon catching snippets of conversation in all of seven common Chinese dialects. He found that his memory of the three lesser-used dialects was rusty. It was easy for him to understand the bits of chatter he heard in the two principal dialects, Mandarin and Cantonese, but had some trouble remembering Hsiang and Wu. By the time he'd struggled to recall the meaning of words spoken in the lesser-used Min, or when the dialect was Kan-Hakka or Yueh, even the main thread of what he overheard was sometimes completely lost.

Nothing in any of the bits of conversations that reached Ki's ears had a great deal of meaning to him. Most of the men passing him were chatting about family matters in the manner of close friends or relatives, though a few were boasting of winnings or complaining of losses at fantan or poker or faro. Moving with the flow of the traffic, Ki followed the pair of men ahead of him when they went into the first large lighted building.

He found himself in a room that took up the entire first floor of the building except for an open area along one wall, where a railing enclosed a stairway that led to the upper floors. Aside from the four gaming tables which occupied the corners, the room was unfurnished and had no distinguishing characteristics unless the oil lamps that hung from the ceiling above each table could be counted as decorative features.

Men were standing three and four deep at the large square

tables. Aside from the operators, who had on dark blue or black American-style business suits, the garb of the gamblers might well have been a uniform, for nine of every ten of them wore the loose dark-colored trousers and blouse common to Chinese laborers or coolies, and their gnarled callused hands also identified them as common laborers.

Ki stopped just inside the door and stepped back against the wall to examine his surroundings. As he scanned the bustling room, he noted immediately that in each corner a large Mongol-type Chinese man was standing. Like the dealers, they had on dark American-style business suits. They kept their eyes fixed on the tables, silently observing the players, obviously keeping watch on the games, ready to move at the first sign of trouble. When he'd absorbed all that was possible from his vantage point, Ki strolled idly from one table to another, taking stock of the games.

All four tables were devoted to fantan, played in the traditional Chinese fashion with counters tossed at random into a large bronze bowl which was emptied into a square marked on the table. Each side of the square was numbered, the winners being those players who had bet on the side with the number corresponding to that of the counters remaining inside it after the game's operator raked the counters out of the center in groups of four. Winners were paid three times the amount of the bets made on a side, but could "straddle" their bets by placing them in a corner; if either of the sides won, the player was paid two-and-a-half times the amount he'd wagered.

Ki had an intimate familiarity with fantan, both in its traditional version and the later European variation. During the first days of his rebellious youth after he'd been banished by his family from Japan, he had haunted the gambling dives in the bustling seaports on both sides of the Yellow Sea. From Fusan to Heijo and around the coast to Lushan in the north, Ki had risked his small allowance on the tables.

Fantan had been the chief gambling game, and at first Ki had lost more often than he'd won. Then, by watching the professional gamblers who haunted the fantan parlors, he'd learned to double his bets and straddle them. By putting this knowledge to use he'd begun winning consistently, parlaying his small stakes into high winnings. After his interest in the martial arts led to his enrolling with the master Hirata, Ki grew so engrossed in perfecting his combat skills that he gave up gambling.

Now, the long-unused mathematics of the straddle and its use began to return as Ki recalled his own experiences. As he moved unobtrusively from one table to the next he could see at once that the operators were professionals, experts at their jobs, and crooked experts at that, putting their skill to work by cheating the inexperienced players. The traditional equipment and method of play made their cheating almost impossible for any but an expert such as Ki to detect.

Wasting neither time nor motion, the operators kept the games going at the fastest possible pace. While the players were placing their bets—all of them small amounts: nickels, dimes, quarters, even a few copper pennies and rarely as much as a half dollar—the operator picked up a handful of the small Chinese copper "cash" pieces, which were used as counters, and dropped them into a bronze bowl. Always a few of the counters were spilled and swept aside; Ki had learned than an operator accustomed to handling any type of counter could judge by their weight in his hand how many he needed to drop into the bowl to assure the smallest number of winning bets.

Swirling the big bowl three or four times, adding a few counters at random with each swirl, the operator dexterously inverted the bowl in the center of the table and lifted it up immediately, leaving the counters strewn on the green felt. With long ivory wands the operators assembled the scattered counters into groups of four and pushed them out of the square. As the number of counters diminished, the players' voices rose in excited chatter until the play ended when there were four or less counters remaining in the square. Then the chatter subsided as winners laughed and losers stood quietly sour-faced while the dealers paid off those who had bet correctly on the winning side.

None of the games lasted more than two or three minutes from the time the bets were laid. Then, as soon as the winning players had been paid off and the losers's stakes whisked away, the operators replenished the bowl of counters while the players placed fresh wagers, and the bowl was upended again. Ki strolled from one table to the next for perhaps a quarter of an hour before climbing the stairs to the second floor.

In layout and furnishings the second floor was a virtual replica of the first, even down to the silent Mongol strong-arm men who stood in each corner of the room impassively watching the tables. Fantan also ruled here, but the tables were much less crowded. On this floor small ivory discs were used as counters and the betting was in twenty-five cent pieces, half dollars, and silver dollars. The rapid pace of play was the same, though the cheating by the operators was done much more skillfully.

In the smaller crowd Ki saw that he would soon become conspicuous if he failed to play. He found an open spot at one of the tables and stepped into it. For his initial bets he laid down single twenty-five cent pieces. After losing the first two straddled bets, he won the next three. The payoff wiped out his losses, and he promptly switched his bets to half dollars when the next game began. He lost the first stake he placed, then began winning consistently enough to get fifty dollars ahead.

At that point Ki started betting dollars, doubling or even tripling his stakes. In an hour or less of play the stacks of big silver cartwheels in front of him grew to impressive dimensions, and Ki began paying closer attention to the game's operator. The man soon laid aside his ivory wand and started to remove the counters with his hand.

Ki waited until the operator palmed an extra counter in addition to the four he should have removed and reached quickly across the table to grasp his closed fist.

"You are cheating," he said loudly.

When a stir of murmurs sounded from the players, Ki put the tip of his thumb on the cluster of flexed muscles between the operator's thumb and forefinger and applied merciless pressure. The man's hand was forced open, and five of the ivory counters instead of four dropped to the table.

Gasps and indignant words of complaint rippled through the onlookers. The operator turned his face toward the guard in the nearest corner and snapped a quick command.

His heavy jaw set menacingly, the Mongol started toward Ki.

Chapter 7

Ki did not move or release the fantan dealer's hand until the advancing Mongol had pushed through the crowd of players running away from the table. Waiting until the guard had reached the corner of the table, Ki yanked the dealer's arm straight and twisted it sharply. When the fantan operator bent at the waist to ease the punishing pressure on his arm and shoulder, Ki brought his foot up into the operator's midsection, and as his *mae-geri-keage* kick went home, he swung the man into a hard collision with the guard. Though the Mongol took a quick backward step, he was too near the operator to avoid the man's hurtling form. He was forced to abandon his attack for a moment while he wrestled with the operator's limp form and freed himself.

That moment was all Ki needed. Whirling as he advanced on the Mongol and adding the momentum of his body to the force of his muscles, he swept his flexed arm in a *migi-tagatana* swipe. Ki's accuracy was unerring. The arc of his swinging arm brought his bent elbow to the exact spot he'd aimed for, high on the side of the Mongol's face. The point of Ki's elbow crashed home with such force that it shattered the big man's high cheekbone and sent him slumping unconscious to the floor.

Even before Ki put the hulking Mongol out of action, the other three guards had started from their corner stations to aid the one who now lay unconscious on the floor. Ki had no doubt that he could handle the three of them, but to do any more damage was not part of the plan he'd formed during the time he'd been playing fantan.

He leaped to the center of the table. It was a risky move because his position now made him an easy target for the pistols that bulged on the hips of the approaching Mongols. Knowing the Oriental mind as he did, Ki had decided quickly that all three of the guards would feel forced to salvage the personal pride, which Orientals call "face," by subduing him without using their weapons.

Ki won his personal gamble. The guards did not reach for their revolvers, but stopped at the table's edge and lurched forward, leaning as far as they could reach and thrusting with clawing hands, trying to trip him or to grab his moving feet. It took all the nimble acrobatics Ki could muster to keep dancing and whirling with enough speed to evade their sweeping lunges, but he managed to dance out of their reach. Then, as he swerved and circled, he began taunting the guards.

"Your *cham* would laugh if he saw you now," he said, speaking in Cantonese, but using the old Mongol word *cham* to describe their boss or leader. "But he would not laugh long. He would be angry because three of you together cannot catch me!"

"You talk too much, coolie!" one of the Mongols panted. "You'll tire soon; then we will grab you!"

"Not soon enough!" Ki shot back. "You will save face if I allow you to take me to your *cham* before I do any more damage."

Although the three frustrated Mongols did not immediately stop their efforts to capture him, Ki saw he'd chosen the right approach and that his warning had gotten home. Their faces showing a mixture of anger and worry, the three Mongols scattered around the table. Each covering a different side, they continued to lunge forward, their sweeping

71

arms outstretched as they tried to grab Ki's ankles, but they were defeated by Ki's ability to move faster than they could, as well as by the size of the table.

For several minutes he eluded them successfully, and after he felt that they had realized the futility of their frantic efforts, Ki began taunting the trio again. He said, "Your clumsiness makes all Mongols lose face! But I will help you. If you agree you will not harm me and take me to your *cham* as though you'd captured me, I will surrender to you."

Ki's offer caused the Mongols to exchange surprised glances, then in Cantonese a bit less fluent than Ki's, one of them asked, "You will give up to us?"

"I will let you save face by surrendering to you, but you must let me save face if I do so," Ki replied promptly while continuing his evasive acrobatics.

"What do you mean?" the guard asked.

"You must let the *cham* judge how I should be treated," Ki answered.

"If we agree to take you to our *cham,* will you give up now and go with us peacefully?" the man asked.

"Yes."

"He will have you punished," the guard warned.

"No, he will thank me."

"Why should he do that?"

"If I tell the coolies who come here to gamble that they are being cheated, they will not come back. That would cost your *cham* a great deal of money," Ki replied, swerving in time to avoid one of the Mongols who lunged for him.

"There is nowhere else the coolies can go to play fantan," the guard said. "They will come back."

"But you won't be here," Ki retorted. "What will you say when the *cham* asks you why you did not capture me at once?"

Again, Ki showed his understanding of the way in which the minds of his fellow Orientals worked. The guard with

72

whom he'd been talking took a half step away from the table.

Speaking in Mongol, the man told his companions, "This fellow speaks with good sense. If the *cham* should come down here and see this—"

"You're right," one of the others agreed. "Let's take his offer and get him upstairs before he does more harm. Then the *cham* cannot blame us for what has happened."

"What about the coolies and the other dealers who've been watching us?" the third asked. "They've seen us fail."

"We can keep them from talking," the first guard replied. "I say we should do what he wants us to." When the other Mongols nodded and stepped back from the table, he turned back to Ki and said, "Come down. We agree, if you will do one thing."

"What's that?" Ki asked.

"You must let the *cham* think we captured you, and say nothing about our agreement."

"How do I know I can trust you?" Ki asked, but he stopped his dancelike moves.

"You have heard what we said," the Mongol replied. "We will fight you no more, and we will take you to the *cham.*"

"Then I will not tell him you couldn't capture me," Ki told the men.

He stopped his circling and dodging and leaped to the floor. The Mongol who had done most of the talking reached to grab his arm, but Ki brushed the man's hand aside. Reacting quickly, the Mongol swept his arm back as though to draw his revolver, but Ki moved with greater swiftness.

Grabbing the Mongol's hand, he held it in an *aiki-jitsu* grip. The iron tips of his fingers curved into a claw that dug into the muscles on the back of the man's hand. His own thumb applied a paralyzing pressure on the opposite side. Though the guard's face twitched for a moment reg-

73

istering the pain that was shooting up his arm, he controlled his expression quickly.

His voice reflecting only a hint of the pain he felt, the Mongol said, "I did not start to harm you, only to hold your arm, so you will look like a captive. If we are to deceive the *cham,* you must let us treat you like a prisoner!"

Ki recognized the truth of the guard's explanation and let his hand drop free. His voice firm, he said, "You can hold my arm. But I will not be gentle with you if you try to trick me!"

"I swear on the bones of my ancestors that we will keep our word," the Mongol replied. "Now, let us go upstairs."

After Ki had started to town, Jessie told Nate, "I don't mean to criticize your housekeeping, but if you're not too tired we ought to do a little cleaning up before it's dark."

"I never was good at neatening up a cabin," Nate grinned a bit shamefacedly. "I'd've readied things up a little bit if I'd knowed you and Ki was going to stay here with me."

"There's plenty of time to do it now," she told him. "I guess there's a spring or a brook close by, but I don't know where it is, so if you'll go after a bucket of water, we'll get started."

"Sure," Nate nodded. "My spring ain't but a step or so away. And I seen there ain't enough firewood to cook breakfast with, so I'll split some while there's still daylight left."

As soon as Nate left for the spring, Jessie busied herself with stripping the blankets from the bunks. She took them outside to air before bedtime and looked at the horses to make sure they were in a safe place for the night. When Nate returned with a full waterbucket, she was back in the cabin, spreading her bedroll on the upper bunk.

Nate said, "Now, don't you go taking a lot of trouble in here, Jessie. I'll just fix me a shakedown on the floor and you and Ki take them bunks."

74

"No," she said firmly. "You'd better take this lower bunk, Nate. Ki won't mind sleeping on a pallet on the floor for the short time we're going to be here."

"Well," Nate said hesitantly, "it don't seem like that's the right way to treat him, but I got to admit the floor's sorta drafty for my old bones. You go ahead and fix things any way you like. I'll get at splitting up the firewood."

In a moment Jessie heard the solid thunking of Nate's axe biting into wood. After putting a fresh chunk of wood in the stove, she filled the kettle and was just returning to the bunk to finish arranging her bedding when the crack of a rifle broke the twilight stillness. Almost as an echo a second shot barked. Grabbing her rifle, Jessie ran toward the cabin door.

Another shot spat from the dense growth and a bullet splintered the door frame as she got outside. She saw Nate sprawled on his face beside the woodpile, but still another rifle spoke from the cover of the pine saplings and its slug kicked up a spurt of dust among the woodchips that strewed the ground inches from where Nate was lying.

Jessie dropped flat and lay motionless, hoping the snipers in the underbrush would think they'd scored a hit, but either her ruse did not fool the unseen attackers or they were determined to make sure, for the next shot from the low pine saplings struck the ground between her and Nate, sending woodchips flying into the air.

This time Jessie had a fix on the location of the sniper and she let off another round in the direction from which the rifle had spoken. When the air grew quiet as the echoes of her shot died away, she called, "Nate! Nate, how badly are you hit?"

"Worse'n I like, but not as bad as them fellers out there might think." Nate's strained voice was filled with pain, and a bloodstain spreading on his faded blue denim shirt told Jessie that he was trying to make the best of a bad situation. He went on, "I got to git back in the cabin and grab my rifle, Jessie. Can you hold 'em till I git back to help you?"

"Go on inside," she replied. "But don't come back out here. Shoot from the windows, like you were doing when Ki and I got here. I'll come in as soon as you're ready to cover me."

While she was answering Nate, Jessie's eyes were scanning the undergrowth, but just as had been the case earlier, the young pines concealed the snipers. Nate began to crawl toward the cabin door, and before he'd quite reached it, one of the hidden attackers let off another round. The slug went high and hit the cabin wall just as Nate put forth a final effort and got through the door.

As Nate scrambled into the cabin, Jessie rolled to the only cover she saw, the woodpile at the cabin's corner. She reached its protection just as a bullet fired at Nate hit the cabin wall above her head. Now Jessie turned her full attention to locating the hidden riflemen. She scanned the wall of green foliage that concealed them, her eyes fixed on the tips of the pine saplings outlined against the darkening sky, watching for them to move.

Her vigilance was repaid almost at once. A line of movement rippled along the tips of the saplings to her right. As nearly as Jessie could tell, whoever was responsible for making the treetops move was advancing on a slant toward the cabin. She studied the tips of the saplings for several moments, trying to place the position of the man on the ground.

When she was as sure as she could be of the moving man's location, Jessie bracketed the area with three quick shots spaced to cover a span of fifteen or twenty yards. She knew that she'd chosen well when a gargled yell of pain rose from the area her shots had covered. A second cry, weaker than the first, came from the spot; the treetops in the area of the cries shook violently for a moment, then were still.

From her left, a good distance from the place where Jessie had fired, a rifle spoke sharply and a slug thudded into the end wall of the cabin. The spot where the bullet plowed into the logs was nowhere near her, and Jessie guessed the man who fired it was shooting blind. Leaping to her feet, she dashed into the cabin. Nate was sprawled on his back on the floor below one of the windows, his rifle lying across his chest, his eyes closed.

For a moment Jessie forgot the attackers outside. She laid her rifle down and dropped to her knees beside Nate. Pressing her palm on his bloodstained shirt, she felt for a heartbeat and found one, a slow but regular pulsing. Jessie breathed more easily then and yanked the placket of his shirt open to expose the bullet wound.

When she finally got Nate's shirt and longjohns pulled away from his chest, Jessie's anxiety subsided still more. The slug had gone in an inch or so below Nate's armpit, leaving a puckered red hole from which a trickle of blood was still flowing, but the flow was not pulsing as would have been the case if the bullet had punctured an artery or gone into a lung.

When Jessie moved her hand around the old prospector's chest to his back, she found no exit wound, but a lump below his shoulderblade told her that the bullet was still buried in his back, under a thin layer of flesh and muscle. Nate stirred and sighed and opened his eyes. When he saw Jessie he managed a wry grin.

In a voice that was weak and trembly, he said, "Looks like I didn't move fast enough, don't it, Jessie?"

"You moved fast enough to save your life," Jessie replied. "Now just lie still, I'll get that wound bandaged."

"But them fellers out there—" Nate began.

"Don't worry," Jessie told him over her shoulder as she

77

located the shirt from which she'd torn the first bandage she'd put on the old prospector. As she ripped more strips from the garment, she went on, "I hit one of them—a lucky shot—but it'll keep the other one busy taking care of him for a while."

"You reckon it's them same fellers that was trying to get me afore you and Ki run 'em off?" Nate asked.

"I'd imagine so, Nate," Jessie replied. "My guess is that they panicked when they saw Ki and me get here. They probably ran a little way, then came back to spy on us. When they saw Ki leave they must've decided that since there were only the two of us left, they'd make another try."

"And they damn near got me, this time," Nate nodded. "They would have, if it hadn't been for you, Jessie."

Jessie was tying the rough bandage she'd pieced together around Nate's chest. She said soberly, "I'm afraid we'll have to give the one who's left another chance at us."

"You mean he's likely watching still?"

"I can't guess what he might be doing, Nate. I know I hit one of them. The other could be watching the cabin or the trail, or he could be on his way back to town with the one I shot."

"Let's just stay holed up and wait 'em out, then," Nate suggested.

Jessie shook her head. "That bullet's still buried in your back, and I don't want to risk trying to cut it out myself. It needs a doctor's attention. We'll have to get into Rough and Ready, but I don't want to risk another gunfight. If the man who shot you is standing watch on the trail somewhere, the odds would be on his side if we ran into him."

"There's a shortcut I use sometimes when I'm in a hurry," Nate told her. "It cuts over some pretty rough ground, and I don't much like to go that way in the dark, but I figure I can make it if you'll give me a little help."

"If the trail's too rough for you to get over on foot, I'll

saddle my horse and you can ride," Jessie said.

"How about them gully shooters out in the brush?"

"I think there's only one left," Jessie replied. "I'm sure I knocked down one of them. The other one might be gone by now, but even if he's not, he'll be busy looking after the one I hit. Besides, it'll be dark by the time we start."

"We'd best get moving, then," Nate told her. His voice was unsteady now. "I reckon you was right about me needing a doctor, Jessie. I'm feeling a mite trembly, but I reckon I can hold on a while longer."

"I'll go saddle up," Jessie said. "The quicker you get to a doctor, the better."

Darkness was almost total by the time Jessie got the horse saddled. Though she kept her rifle within easy reach while she worked, there were no more shots from the saplings beyond the trail. Getting Nate boosted into the saddle took a bit of time, but she set her jaw and used her considerable strength to the utmost, and finally they were ready to set out.

As Jessie led the horse around the cabin, Nate said, "I sure wish I hadn't had to sell my little jackass. It just don't seem right for me to be riding while a lady walks."

"Stop worrying about me, Nate," Jessie replied. "This isn't the first time I've walked and led a horse."

"Sure," the old man replied. "And maybe by the time the doctor gits done with me, we'll run into Ki. I wonder how he's doing right now."

"Ki can take care of himself," Jessie said. "Now, all I want you to think about is keeping me on the right trail."

"Rough and Ready ain't all that big of a town," Nate went on, "and I don't figure Ki'd have to spend much time looking over that place where them Chinks has settled."

Jessie saw that there was only one way to silence the old miner and force him to conserve his strength for the rough trip that lay ahead. She said, "You're right, Nate. Just as

79

soon as I get you to the doctor, I'll look around town and see if I can find him."

At the moment Jessie spoke of him, Ki was mounting the stairs of the gambling house in the Chinese settlement, the Mongol guards behind him. The third floor landing was small and dimly lighted. Three doors opened from it, and one of the guards reached past Ki to tap at the one in the center.

To Ki's surprise, a woman opened the door. He could see her only in silhouette outlined by the bright light that streamed from the room beyond, and he was even more surprised when she spoke to the guards in Cantonese with a pronounced Japanese intonation.

"I have been expecting you," she said. "Yen Shou, you and Chen Hu go back to your places. Fan Shing, you will remain outside my door. I wish to talk to this man alone."

Chapter 8

Ki kept his face impassive. He did not show his surprise at the manner in which he'd been received or by his discovery that a woman fluent in Cantonese was in charge of the gambling house. He stepped into the room and the woman closed the door behind him. She turned toward him then, and when he saw her face in the light for the first time, Ki's earlier surprises were magnified a hundred times.

Facing him was a woman whose features displayed many of the signs of mixed Anglo-Saxon and Oriental blood. Her eyes, nose, cheekbones, in fact the total cast of her face was startlingly similar to the face Ki saw when he looked at himself in a mirror.

For a long moment the woman stood impassively under Ki's scrutiny; then she said, "You will find any of the chairs comfortable. Please sit down. I am brewing tea, which we will sip while we talk. And you may call me Omachi."

"I am Ki," he replied.

When Omachi heard Ki's reply she questioned him silently, with an arching of her thin high-set eyebrows. Years of stern self-discipline enabled Ki to maintain his poise. He did not try to reply to the question implied by Omachi's raised eyebrows, nor had he shown surprise at her appearance. The same rigid self-control dictated his next move. Nodding as though receiving an invitation to drink tea with a strange woman was an everyday occurrence, he selected a chair and settled down, waiting for her to make the first move.

Omachi seemed in no hurry. She studied Ki as closely as he was studying her before moving to a lacquered table on one side of the room and busying herself with a large teapot and cups.

While she worked Ki took the opportunity Omachi was offering him to study her. He'd been unable to tell her age during the quick glance he'd gotten on entering the room, but when she glanced at him over her shoulder while she set the tea to steeping he realized that as with most women of the Orient her features would not change and facial wrinkles would not form until she was in her late sixties. She wore a floor-length kimono held at the throat by a large jade brooch, and because of the loose garment Ki could not tell whether her figure was slight or sturdy.

Perhaps as part of her Anglo-Saxon heritage, Omachi was taller than the average Oriental woman, almost as tall as Ki. She moved with the unstudied grace which typifies most females from the Far East. Her hands were slim, with long fingers and polished, long nails. She wore her coarse black hair in the old Japanese style, in a large loose roll or puff above her forehead with a high bun rising behind it.

Because Omachi's back was toward him most of the time, Ki got only fleeting glimpses of her features, but he remembered them well enough to re-create them in his mind. His memory told him that it was either English or American lineage which showed in her face. It was thin and oval rather than full and round, and her mixed parentage was also revealed by her thin nose, more prominent on her high-cheeked face than it would be on the face of a woman with full Oriental blood.

As Omachi continued to work at preparing their tea, Ki used the time to examine the room. In its simplicity it might have been any of the hundreds of rooms he'd seen in his

82

native Japan. The room was small, but seemed larger than it was because it contained only five pieces of furniture.

There were three chairs arranged in a rough triangle with their backs to a single high window, a table beside which Omachi stood, and a smaller lower table that occupied the space between the chairs. He recognized the carpet as a priceless one, and the *nishi-ki* painting on raw silk that adorned the wall opposite the window as one from the Tokugawa period. A lamp with an etched glass chimney hung from the center of the ceiling and doors on each of the side walls indicated that other rooms adjoined the small chamber.

Finished at last, Omachi lifted a tray on which she'd placed the teapot and two small cups without handles. She carried it to the low table between the chairs and sat down in the chair nearest Ki.

"I hope you've adopted American customs," she said. "Don't expect me to go through the tea ceremony or even to speak Japanese."

"I expect nothing," Ki told her. "But I am certainly more surprised than you are. When you opened the door, you said you were expecting me. Was that to impress your Mongols, or me?"

"A bit of both, I suppose," she replied, pouring tea. "I knew you could not win your fight with the Mongols, but I expected them to kill you."

Ki masked his surprise when he saw his hastily formed plan going up in smoke. He asked Omachi, "You saw the fight?"

"Of course."

"How? If you'd been downstairs, I would have seen you."

After a thoughtful pause, she replied, "I see no harm in telling you. If you prove suitable for my purposes, you will say nothing. If you don't, I have only to call the Mongols,

83

and this time they will kill you."

His face still expressionless, Ki said with matter-of-fact coolness, "I defeated them downstairs. I can defeat them again up here."

"Don't be too sure," she replied. "You did not defeat the Mongols. Even though I couldn't hear, I could see that you persuaded them to stop fighting."

"You could see us, but couldn't hear us?"

Omachi nodded. "But it took only a little imagination for me to guess what you were saying to them."

A challenge in his voice, Ki asked, "What do you think I was telling them?"

"That they were losing face by failing to bring you down from the table where you were dancing. Then you offered to stop fighting if they would take you to their employer."

In spite of wondering for a passing moment how Omachi could have guessed his words so accurately, Ki's initial surprise was evaporating now. He began to plan ahead once more, and to give himself more time, he said, "You were going to show me how it's possible for you to be so well-informed about what happened in the gambling room."

"It's very simple," Omachi replied, standing up.

She moved to the wall hanging and lifted one corner of the silk fabric to reveal a foot-square wooden panel. Ki rose and joined her. Omachi swung the panel to one side and in a slanting recessed mirror he saw the gambling room reflected in miniature from a similar mirror, its surface parallel with the one at which he was looking. It had been concealed in the wall of the downstairs chamber.

In the gambling room, order had been restored by now. Many of the players had returned to the tables, the fantan operators were in their places, and two of the Mongol guards were visible in the room's corners. Ki watched for a moment before turning back to face Omachi.

"A very ingenious arrangement, Omachi," he told her. "I'm familiar with its principles, but have not seen it used before."

"It has been useful to me many times," she said, closing the panel and letting the tapestry fall back into place. "But our tea is getting cool. Let's enjoy it while we talk."

At his first sip of the dark, full-bodied tea, Ki wondered immediately if Omachi was subtly using the beverage to send him a message. He had recognized the tea at once; it was a heavy Kwan Yen from Amoy. Ki knew that tea had several names in the Orient, all of which translated into English as *Iron Goddess of Mercy*. Realizing more clearly than before that he was now facing a woman who could be either a dangerous enemy or a valuable ally, Ki decided to forego the Oriental habit of polite verbal sparring to gain an early advantage over an adversary in a bargaining session. He went to the point at once.

"Your Kwan Yen is excellent," he said. "But I am curious to know why you chose to serve it instead of another blend."

A smile flicked across Omachi's full red lips. "I wondered if you would recognize its flavor. But if the tea has a message, we can talk about that later. I am as curious as you are, Ki. Tell me why you came here; then perhaps I will satisfy your curiosity."

"And shall we both speak the truth?" Ki asked.

"I promise you this, Ki," she replied after a momentary hesitation. "If you ask questions I cannot answer truthfully, I will remain silent, but I will tell you no lies."

"Then I will do the same," Ki said. "Now, where will we start?"

"Wouldn't the best place to start be for you to tell me why you came here?" she asked.

Ki shrugged as he answered truthfully, "I came to satisfy my curiosity when I learned there were Chinese working at

85

building gold dredges somewhere near here."

A near frown rippled across Omachi's high brow. She asked, "You have seen this?"

"No. But I do not doubt the words of the one who told me he has seen them."

"Why should you be interested?"

"I'm interested in many things," Ki evaded.

"Things other than gold dredges?"

"Of course. There are many things of value besides gold."

Ki's finely honed instinct was telling him that he might have discovered in Omachi a rich lode of information, but the same instinct also told him that she was not going to allow him to avoid the long seige of polite double-veiled talk that marks an Oriental bargaining session. He decided to be as vague as possible.

"You're looking for work?" she asked.

"Perhaps. Perhaps not."

"That's not an answer," Omachi frowned. This time she made no effort to stop her forehead from wrinkling.

"It's the only one I can give you," Ki told her.

"Then I will ask you in a different way," she said quickly. "Did you come to here tonight looking for work?"

Ki shook his head. "No, I'm looking for information."

"Information about what?"

"As I told you, I am interested in many things."

"And have you found the information you're after?"

"Not all that I need—at least not yet. But I'm sure now that I've come to the right place to look."

"Explain, please," Omachi said.

"I'm not sure that I can," Ki replied slowly. When Omachi did not speak, but arched her eyebrows questioningly again, Ki went on, "Since we seem to have reached a point where you have no more questions ready, let me ask you about things that I find puzzling."

"That's fair," Omachi nodded. "Ask me."

"How did a woman of your youth and beauty become the *cham* of such a large gambling establishment?"

Omachi was silent for a long moment before she replied, "Even though your compliment is as sweet to my ears as honey to my mouth, your question is one that I cannot answer."

"Then we're getting nowhere," Ki observed.

"At least that's one thing we can agree on," Omachi said. She was silent for a moment; then she stood up. "Come with me, Ki. Perhaps there is a path we can follow that will help us to agree on other things more readily."

Ki followed Omachi to the door in a side wall. She opened it and led him into the adjoining room. It was even smaller than the one they had left, more sparsely furnished, and warm almost to the point of being overheated.

Mirrors covered the walls that flanked the doorway. They reflected a subdued glow from a circle of coals shining red around the rim of a small kettle that stood on a charcoal brazier, lighting the room with a twilight dimness. A large Japanese bed, raised only a few inches from the floor, occupied the center of the chamber, and low tables on each side of the bed completed its furnishings.

"A man and a woman can talk freely only when they know each other well," Omachi said. Indicating the bed, she went on, "And there is no better place to become acquainted."

"No," Ki agreed. He controlled the twitching that was beginning to bring him erect after a long period of abstinence and kept himself flaccid. Then he replied to Omachi by quoting an aphorism. "An hour in bed will bring a man and woman closer than a year of talk."

"Then let us begin to become closer," Omachi said. She unpinned the brooch at the high neck of her kimono and shrugged her shoulders to start the garment sliding to the floor.

87

In the warm light shed by the reflected coals, Ki's appreciative glance of Omachi's shapely figure did not keep him from noticing that she showed her mixed blood in her body as well as her facial features. Her shoulders were broad as befitted a woman of her stature, and her breasts larger than those of most Oriental women. The puckered rosettes at their tips glowed a soft reddish tan, and though her pubic brush was scanty her hips were wide and tapered down to full rounded thighs. When Ki glanced at her back reflected in the mirror, he saw that her buttocks were firm and as round as twin pillows.

"You are shy," Omachi smiled as Ki stood looking at her, but he made no move to start undressing. "I see that I must help you."

Moving close to Ki, she unbuttoned his loose cotton jacket and let it fall to the floor. When she saw the breadth of his chest and its layered muscles, she ran her hand softly over their rippled firmness and then stroked the smooth bulges that swelled from his upper arms.

Ki loosened the knot of the *surushin* he wore as a belt, and the weight of the lead balls at the ends of the braided horse-hair rope pulled it to the floor. Then he pushed his trousers and the wide folds of the undergarment he wore beneath them down his hips and let them fall to the floor together.

Omachi trailed her hand down Ki's sides to his groin and cradled his limp sex in her soft palms. "You're not too eager," she said. "That's very good. Come, let me attend to you."

Ki followed her to the brazier. Omachi paused beside one of the low tables long enough to pick up a folded cloth and dipped it into the kettle. She squeezed the cloth to distribute the water and passed it gently over his hips and crotch. Letting the cloth drop to the floor, she straightened up and gestured to the bed. Then she took Ki's hand and led him to its side.

"It's waiting for us," she said softly. "And even if you're not yet ready, I'll soon take care of that."

Omachi waited until Ki laid down and stretched out, then knelt on the wide bed beside him. She bent over and rubbed her cheek softly along his chest and the corded muscles of his flat abdomen, then turned her head to nibble at his smooth skin with gentle nips of her full lips. Ki lay quietly, enjoying Omachi's expert caresses, and released his control enough to allow his flaccid shaft to begin swelling slowly.

Omachi did not stop her caresses when her lips reached Ki's groin. She let her tongue ripple slowly along his beginning erection before engulfing it with her mouth. Ki responded to the gentle rasping of her agile tongue by allowing himself to swell to a full erection. Omachi continued her caresses until she'd brought him fully rigid, then lifted her head, releasing him.

Sitting back on her heels, she looked admiringly at what her caresses had brought to life and said, "I promised to take care of you. Now you are ready to take care of me."

Ki lost no time in responding when Omachi stretched out on the bed beside him. He lifted himself above her and Omachi brought her knees up until they were almost to her shoulders and spread her thighs in readiness to receive him. Her hand snaked down to grasp his firm cylinder of rigid flesh and guide it to her crotch. Ki thrust into her and Omachi gasped in response to his deep lunging penetration.

Ki did not begin stroking at once. He pressed his pubic arch against her and held himself there firmly while he bent his head to find the protruding nipples of her fully budded breasts with his lips. He moved from one mound to the other, pulling Omachi's pebbled rosettes into his mouth with a gentle suction as he passed his tongue in hard quick flicks over their swollen tips. He felt Omachi's inner muscles close on his shaft and grasp it, and only then did he start a slow measured stroking.

As Ki continued his long slow thrusts, Omachi arched her back, twisting her shoulders from side to side, lifting and rotating her hips. Her body grew taut; she threw her head back and closed her eyes. Ki prolonged his tongue caresses and his leisurely strokes until he felt Omachi begin to quiver. Then he began to thrust faster. He drove into her with ramrod lunges, deep swift penetrations, while Omachi's body began to ripple and moans of her delight burst from her throat.

After a few minutes of Ki's lusty driving, Omachi passed the point of no return. She cried out loudly as her body shook and her hips gyrated wildly. Her muscles tensed and her cries rose to a crescendo. Then Ki felt the tension drain from her body as her loud outcries faded to moans and then to silence, and after a final quivering shudder she lay limp and quiet.

Even then, Ki did not stop stroking. He slowed the tempo of his thrusts, but continued to penetrate her with the full length of his still swollen shaft while Omachi lay motionless. Her body soon grew taut again, and now Ki speeded up. He was almost ready to release himself in his own climax, but held his urge in control until Omachi began rising for the second time to the peak of passion, writhing and rocking her hips in rhythm with his deep lunges.

She reached the summit more quickly now, and Ki increased the speed of his steady thrusting until Omachi's gasping moans told him she was entering another climax. He let himself go at last, jetting as he drove hard with a few final lunges. Omachi's throaty outbursts began again while she twisted and tossed frantically beneath him. Ki waited until she'd passed into the ebbing moments of her climax before he stopped and allowed himself to relax on her soft, trembling body.

Omachi broke the silence that had settled on the room when her cries of satisfaction died away. She said, "You're as lusty a lover as I thought you'd be when I watched you in the mirror. Was your pleasure as great as mine?"

"Of course, it was," he replied. "So much that I am ready to repeat it when you are."

"This soon?"

"Why not?" Ki asked. He began flexing the muscles in his buttocks to bring himself fully erect more quickly.

Omachi stirred and said, "When I feel you begin to swell, as I do now, I know you must mean what you say. Once more, then, and afterward we will talk. I have a great deal to say to you, Ki. It may be that you are the man I've been waiting for."

Chapter 9

"Your father is a very lucky man," the doctor told Jessie as he held up the mushroom-shaped lead slug he'd just taken from Nate's back. "This bullet hit his ribs and they deflected it around the bone. If it had hit him a bit more toward the center of his body it would have gone through his heart."

Nate lay face-down on the operating table in the doctor's office, a wide, fresh white bandage encircling his chest below the armpits. He was still unconscious from the chloroform administered by the young doctor before cutting out the bullet.

Jessie had stopped at the first doctor's office she'd seen when she and Nate reached Rough and Ready. Luckily, there'd been no patients waiting, and Dr. Perry had been able to attend to the old man's wound at once.

"Yes, Nate's lucky, I'll agree," Jessie nodded, looking at the unconscious man. "But he's not my father, Dr. Perry, just an old family friend. I was visiting him when two men attacked his cabin."

"A prospector, I think you said?" Dr. Perry asked. When Jessie nodded, he went on, "I guess some crook heard a rumor that your friend had made a good strike and was trying to steal his gold."

Jessie did not bother to correct the doctor's guess. She asked, "Will Nate be unconscious long?"

"Another half hour, perhaps a bit longer. He'll be all

92

right, of course. If he'd been a younger man, I'd have removed this bullet without giving him chloroform, but he's pretty well up in years."

"Will he have to stay here, or can I take him back to his cabin when he comes to?"

"That's going to depend on how he feels when the chloroform wears off, but I don't think a short horseback ride will hurt him, as long as he's careful."

"Can he just stay here until he's conscious, then?" Jessie asked.

"Of course. It's not quite eight o'clock, and it's not likely I'll have any more emergencies until the men in town start getting wild around midnight. When they get a little drunk there'll be a few broken noses and probably another bullet wound or a knife cut for me to take care of."

"It sounds to me as though Rough and Ready lives up to its name," Jessie commented.

"It does, Miss—"

"Starbuck," she said when the doctor paused. "Jessie Starbuck. And don't bother asking Nate to pay you when he comes to. I'll take care of the bill right now, if you'll tell me how much it is."

Perry glanced at the clock on his office wall and said, "Well, it still isn't ten o'clock; that's when my fee goes up. An office visit is two dollars and I'll have to charge another dollar-fifty for the chloroform and bandage."

"Suppose I give you ten dollars, Dr. Perry," Jessie said. "If Nate needs to come back for a second time to get a fresh bandage or something like that, you'll have been paid for it."

"If that's what you want to do, Miss Starbuck. You'll be coming back for him, I suppose?"

"Yes, of course. I'll see that he gets home safely."

"Do you have a place where you can wait?"

Jessie shook her head. "No. But I haven't had any supper

93

yet, and I've an errand to take care of while I'm in town. I'll find a restaurant, and if Nate's still unconscious when I get back after supper I'll wait here in your office until he's ready to go to his cabin."

"Would you mind if I make a suggestion, Miss Starbuck?" the young doctor asked.

"Certainly not."

"As you said a minute ago, Rough and Ready lives up to its reputation. By this time of the evening all the town's decent women are at home, and I'm afraid you might run into some kind of trouble if you go out on the street alone. Now, I haven't eaten yet, and since your friend here won't move for at least another hour, I'd like to invite you to have supper with me."

Jessie studied Perry's face for a moment. In her concern for Nate, this was the first time she'd really looked at him closely, though she'd been impressed by the quick competence he'd shown in treating the wound. Doctor Perry was still on the short side of forty, though the short neatly trimmed beard he wore in deference to the day's professional custom made him look older. She reached a decision quickly.

"I'd like that very much, Dr. Perry, if you're sure it's safe for Nate to be here alone," she replied.

"That table has a belt attached to keep anyone from falling off," he told Jessie. "I'll fasten it and lock the door when we leave. I'm sure everybody in town knows there isn't anything in my office worth stealing, and your horse will be all right while we're away."

"In that case, I'd enjoy very much having your company at supper," Jessie replied. "Even though it'll be a hurried meal, I don't really enjoy eating alone."

"You said you wanted to talk," Ki reminded Omachi.

They were lying side by side in exhausted relaxation, their naked bodies bathed in the gentle heat radiated by the

94

brazier. Ki had begun to wonder if Omachi had fallen asleep, as her eyes had been closed for several minutes. She opened them now. Ignoring her nudity, she propped herself up on an elbow and looked at him.

"I said more than that," she reminded him. "I told you I wonder if you're the man I've been trying to find. Are you, Ki?"

"Suppose you tell me what you're looking for," he countered.

Omachi replied promptly, "I already know two important things that should help us work well together. You're a very satisfactory lover, and you won't look down on me because of my mixed blood, since yours is the same mixture as mine."

"I can see why you'd consider both of them important," Ki told her. "But there must be other things as well."

This time, Omachi did not answer so quickly. After a few moments of silence, she replied, "Added to your accepting me for what I am, you've also passed two more of my tests. You know how to fight hard, but you also know how to win just by talking. That only leaves two and a half more."

"Two and a half?" Ki smiled, raising his brows as he asked the question.

"Yes. One is that you must want to be very rich. The other is that you must agree to stay with me after we're rich. Since I've been in America, I've seen many men new to riches, Ki, and most of them leave a wife who's helped them to get rich and find another woman who's younger and more beautiful."

"And the half?"

"That goes with our mixed blood. We will both think the same way."

"Your tests certainly aren't ordinary," Ki said. He realized a bit belatedly that she had suddenly changed from a pliant sexual siren to a very serious business woman.

"Perhaps not," she told him. "But you're the first man I've seen who I think might be the one I'm after. Are you?"

Choosing his words carefully, Ki replied, "I can't say, Omachi. I can only guess your reasons for wanting this man you're looking for, and that's not enough to let me judge."

This time Omachi was not as quick to answer. She finally said, "Ki, a little while ago you asked me a question that I did not answer. Now, I will answer it. Perhaps if I do it will help you to understand better what I want."

"Are you sure that's a good idea?"

"It may not be. But I hope you will understand."

"Go ahead, then."

"You know of the Yoshiwara in Tokyo?" Omachi asked.

"Of course," Ki nodded. "In this country it would be called a red light district."

Omachi spoke rapidly, her voice flat and expressionless, watching Ki's face expectantly. "When I was fifteen, my parents sold me to a man in the Yoshiwara to work as a whore. I was there for seven years." She paused, waiting for him to comment. When his expression did not change and he said nothing, she went on, "I pleased one of my customers so greatly that he bought me from the owner of the house where I worked. He was a samurai, very old and very rich. He soon grew tired of me, but instead of selling me to someone else he kept me to offer his guests. There were many men who visited him, not Japanese, some from countries I had not known about before. I learned a great deal from them."

"Pillow talk?" Ki asked when Omachi paused again.

"Certainly," she nodded. "Even in the Yoshiwara I learned that men who are too old to satisfy a woman in bed like to boast of other things in which they have succeeded."

A suspicion had begun forming in Ki's mind when Omachi told him of her samurai owner's guests. He asked, "These guests of the samurai were all old men, then?"

"Most of them were," she nodded. "Some were even older than the samurai."

"Is there more to your story?" Ki asked.

"A great deal more. After several years one of the men who was a frequent visitor bought me from the old samurai and took me with him to Germany. He was much older than the samurai and soon grew so feeble that even the skills I had learned in the Yoshiwara could not arouse him. Soon after the German understood that he could get no more pleasure from me, he gave me to a Frenchman, who passed me on to an American."

Ki's suspicion had become almost a certainty as he listened to Omachi's story. He asked her, "Were these men associated in business with your samurai, Omachi?"

"They were and still are," she nodded. "In many kinds of business. All of them own large important companies, manufacturing plants, much land, banks, and things of that sort."

"Always in their own countries?" Ki asked, keeping his voice casual.

"That was usually so when the samurai first bought me. But soon I saw that even though his visitors were old and rich, they wanted to make themselves still richer. When they learned of the great wealth of this country, they began buying land and businesses in America."

"Let me ask you something, Omachi," Ki said. Though he was positive by now that the organization she described could only be the cartel, he wanted to be absolutely sure that his suspicions were correct. "Are all the businesses these men own legal?"

"At first, they were. Not now. That's how I came to be here, because of what I learned during my years in the underworld of the Yoshiwara."

"So this gambling house you run belongs to someone else?"

"Not only this one, but others in different places. When

97

my employer and his friends decided to build gold dredges, they also started other buildings as well."

"What other buildings," Ki inquired.

"When the dredges begin to produce gold, there will be a new gold rush to the Mother Lode. My employers have set up these gambling houses and many others. New brothels, too. I am in charge of them as well as some of the gambling houses in small out-of-the way places like Rough and Ready."

"It sounds to me like you have a very responsible position with a large organization," Ki observed. "Will you go a step further and tell me why you're looking for a man to help you? It seems to me that your organization should have enough men to provide one for you."

Omachi's reply did not come quickly this time. She studied Ki's face closely for several moments before deciding to go on, then said, "I don't want a man for the organization, Ki. I'm going to be the slave who revolts against the master."

"That sounds like you're planning to go into business for yourself," Ki frowned.

"Yes. When the new gold rush starts here in the Mother Lode, I can make a fortune quickly. But I must start at once. Already there is someone else who has seen the same opportunity, but I am sure she does not have the knowledge I have."

"She?" Ki asked. "Another woman?"

Omachi nodded. "Her name is Jessie Starbuck. Somehow she learned about the big new dredges and has been going through the Mother Lode buying small claims from prospectors."

In spite of Ki's bewilderment, he kept his face impassive. He asked Omachi, "How long has she been doing this?"

"Three months or more. I learned about her only a few weeks ago when one of the prospectors who had sold his claim on Dutch Flat told one of the women in the brothel I manage there."

"You've never seen her, then?"

"No. But if this Jessie Starbuck has the same plan I've worked out, I must stop her and begin buying claims myself."

"How did this woman find out about the dredges?"

"I haven't learned that yet. And it's not important. You can find her and kill her as soon as we begin our own work. I've heard she's in the Calaveras country now. You can pick up her trail very easily."

Ki saw at once that Omachi was quite serious. To gain time, he asked, "What will the heads of your organization do when you tell them you want to leave?"

Omachi shrugged. "I won't tell them, of course. I'll just disappear. If they should be angry enough, I'm quite sure they will order one of their assassins to kill me. That's why I need a man who thinks quickly and fights skillfully and without fear."

"You flatter me," Ki said.

"I describe you correctly," she replied. "Will you decide to become a rich man and join me, Ki?"

Because Omachi had not recognized his name at the outset, Ki was positive by now that she was not high enough in the ranks of the cartel to know a great deal about its longstanding battle with Jessie. He had often heard Alex Starbuck remark that the cartel was like an octopus, its tentacles operating independently, controlled by a brain that, like the creature's head, was small in comparison to its total bulk.

Weighing the odds quickly, Ki decided that even if he were successful in getting more information from Omachi, what he might learn was less important than finding the false Jessie Starbuck and putting a stop to her activities.

He said, "No, Omachi. I will not take your offer."

"Why? Surely you're not afraid?" When Ki shook his head, she pressed, "Is it because you don't want to be led by a woman? Or because my caresses didn't please you?"

"No," Ki replied. Then he said truthfully, "Great wealth

99

doesn't tempt me. The man you need is one who wants to be rich."

"I have always thought that all men want riches," Omachi said. "But I see that I've misjudged you. A pity. Now I will have to tell the Mongols to kill you."

Ki had anticipated Omachi's reaction. He stiffened the three first fingers of his hand and jabbed them with the speed of a lightning bolt into the soft flesh behind her jawbone. His blow was delivered with the precise control that only a master of the martial arts can achieve. Omachi gave a single convulsive shudder as the blow instantly brought on almost total paralysis. Her jaw fell slack and her eyes turned upward as she lapsed into unconsciousness.

Ki stopped long enough to press his hand on her bare breast and feel her heartbeat. He did not want to kill her, as such a jab would do if administered with too much force. Her heart was pulsing slowly but steadily, and he knew that it would return to normal within ten minutes or less. He dressed quickly and hurried to the door leading to the stairs. The Mongol guard was still standing, waiting at the top of the steps.

"Your *cham* told me to tell you to go back to your job," Ki told the man. "I'm doing an errand for her and will be back very soon. She does not want to be interrupted, and you and the other guards will appear not to notice me when I come back."

To Ki's relief, the Mongol accepted the explanation with a nod and silently followed him downstairs. Ki breathed more freely when he got outside the gambling house, and as soon as he was out of sight in the darkness he quickened his pace as he wound through the twisting streets of the settlement. As the last of its houses were behind him, he started at an easy distance-eating trot toward Rough and Ready.

•   •   •

Doctor Perry stood aside to let Jessie leave the cafe first, then followed her into the semidarkness of the street. Like most of the mining towns in the Mother Lode, Rough and Ready had no street lights. Oil lamps from the stores and saloons made rectangular checkerboards of the dirt streets. They glowed as rectangles of semibrightness between strips of darkness.

As they started toward the doctor's office, Jessie said, "I enjoyed our dinner very much, Doctor, but I do wish you hadn't insisted on me being your guest. That wasn't in my mind when I asked you about a place to eat."

"I have very few pleasures in this town, Miss Starbuck," Perry said. "Enjoying a meal with a charming lady hasn't been among them until now."

"Have you been practicing here very long?" she asked.

"I sometimes think I've been here too long," the doctor replied. "But it's actually been only a little more than two years."

"I get a feeling that you don't especially like it here," Jessie said as they turned the corner into the street where Perry's office was located. It was darker here than on the main street, the only light was from the lamp the doctor had left burning in his wating room when they left for supper.

"My instructors at the Kansas Medical College as well as the doctors at the hospital in Topeka where I served my internship both advised me to set up my first practice in a small town on the frontier," Perry replied. "They said a year or two of practice in such a place would give me more experience than another five years as an intern."

"Then you'll be going to a city soon, I suppose?" Jessie asked as they stopped in front of the office door while Perry fumbled in his pocket for the key.

"Very soon, I hope," he told her. "In another—"

He stopped as footsteps and the heavier crunching of

hooves on gravel sounded from the street. They turned to look as a man leading a horse approached.

"It seems I'm getting back just in time," Perry said. "If I'm right, that'll be somebody bringing in an injured miner."

In the gloom Jessie could see little more than the outline of the man and the two horses he was leading. He stopped a yard or so from the office door.

"You're the doctor, ain't you?" he asked.

"Yes," Perry replied. "What's your trouble?"

"I got a bad shot-up man here, doc," the new arrival said. "I ain't real sure he's still alive, but he was when I got off my nag and looked at him a few minutes ago, when we got to where there was light enough to see by."

"I'll take care of him at once," Dr. Perry said. "Just wait until I open the door so we'll have more light to see by."

When the doctor opened the office door, light from the lamp poured into the street. Jessie saw the limp form of a man draped over one of the horses. She got only a fleeting glimpse, for as she turned the light struck her face and the newcomer loosed an angry growl.

"Hell's bells!" he snarled. "You're that damn Starbuck woman from out at Nate Wheeler's claim! It was you shot my partner, you dirty bitch!"

Whirling as he dropped the reins he was holding, the man grabbed for the pistol holstered low on his hip.

At the man's first blasphemous shout, Jessie's hand had begun moving toward her Colt. She drew and fired. The newcomer's weapon barked, an instant echo to Jessie's shot.

Chapter 10

Jessie's shot went home a second before her attacker's finger closed on the trigger of his pistol. Though he was sagging when the gun in his hand barked, the slug whistled past Jessie's face so closely that she could feel its breeze and it thudded into the door frame inches from where the doctor stood. He turned around, his mouth agape, in time to see Jessie's assailant sink to the ground.

"What on earth's happening?" Perry asked.

"That man tried to kill me," Jessie replied calmly. "I saw him start to draw and got my own gun out first."

"Is he dead?"

"I'm sure he is." Jessie's voice was level and emotionless. "I'm a reasonably good shot, Dr. Perry."

Both Jessie and the doctor turned toward the door when Nate's voice broke the silence that followed. They saw the old prospector clinging to the jamb.

"Was I you, Doc, I'd take Jessie's word about her shooting," Nate said drily. "I got a hunch that fellow draped over the horse there is one of the rapscallions that was trying to kill me out at my cabin. It was Jessie that picked him off in the brush, and I'd imagine she's finished off his partner now."

Jessie asked, "Are you all right, Nate?"

"Well, I'm a mite wobbly and I feel like a mule kicked me in my side, but I figure to make it," he replied.

Dr. Perry dropped to a knee beside the man who'd tried to kill Jessie and felt for a pulse. He stood up, saying, "He's dead." Then he turned to Jessie and went on, "I'll confess that I don't understand what this is all about. Just who are you, Miss Starbuck?"

Jessie evaded his question by saying, "As I told you, I'm a friend of Nate's, here visiting him."

Before the doctor could ask Jessie more questions, Nate broke in to say, "Jessie didn't have nothing to do with this mess, Doc. A little while back I lost a wad of money bigger'n I could handle to that Blue Star Casino over on Main Street, and it's dollars to doughnuts that the gambler who runs the place sent them two dead fellers out to my cabin to collect it. Jessie got there when they was after me the first time, and then they come back for another try at me."

"That's when the man on the horse got shot," Jessie volunteered. "I'm sure I hit him when they made their second attack."

"I'd forgotten about the other man," Dr. Perry said. "The one Miss Starbuck shot said his friend was pretty bad off." Stepping over to the man draped across the horse, he felt for a heartbeat, but he turned away shaking his head and announced, "This one's dead, too."

"Good riddance," Nate said unfeelingly. "Just two less rapscallions the town's got to worry about."

"I suppose you're right," Perry nodded. "And I'm sure you and Miss Starbuck won't be blamed for defending yourselves. I'll have to report this to the town marshal, though. He'll take care of their horses and gear and see to them being buried."

"I'd have thought someone would have been here by now to see what those shots were all about," Jessie commented, looking both ways along the dark, deserted street.

Nate said, "Shucks, Jessie, if the folks here stop to go

find out about every shot that they hear, nobody'd get any work or gambling done. Was you to've let off ten shots, somebody might've thought it was serious, but two shots ain't nothing."

"I'm afraid he's right, Miss Starbuck," Dr. Perry nodded. "As you remarked at dinner, Rough and Ready lives up to its name." He glanced at the dead men and their horses and went on, "I suppose the best thing for me to do is put the man on the ground across his horse and take both bodies to the marshal's office. I can see that Nate doesn't need any more attention."

As Perry started toward the dead man, Jessie said, "Nate, you get on my horse. We'll go with the doctor as far as the livery stable and rent a horse for you to ride back to your cabin. There's no use in riding double again."

"Oh, shucks, Jessie, I can hoof it back home," Nate protested. "There ain't nothing wrong with my legs."

"You'd better do as Miss Starbuck says," Perry told the old man. "And take things easy for a few days. Come back and see me in a week, and I'll take those stitches out for you."

"Whatever you say, Doc," Nate said resignedly. "But since it'll be easier for me to lead them spare horses than for you or Jessie to, just hand me the reins when I mount up, and we'll be on our way."

Though the streets of Rough and Ready were busy, the men who jostled along the wooden sidewalks paid little attention to Nate and the grisly figures draped over the horses he led. At the marshal's office, Dr. Perry hitched the animals to the rail to save Nate the discomfort of dismounting, and after an exchange of good-byes, he went inside while Jessie and Nate continued to the livery stable. Nate held a tight rein on his mount to keep pace with Jessie's easy strides as they covered the short distance remaining.

"I'm real glad to have your business, ma'am," the liveryman commented. He eyed Nate's bloodstained shirt with undisguised curiosity as he led up the rented horse he'd just finished saddling for Jessie. "You and that Chinee fellow both."

"His name is Ki, and he's Japanese," Jessie replied.

"Japs, Chinks, they're all the same to me," the liveryman shrugged. "Not butting into your business none, but he stopped off a while ago and left his horse for me to feed and look after while he took care of some business he had in town."

"Thank you," Jessie replied coolly. "I know Ki had some errands to take care of. He'll be back for the horse when he's finished them."

"Oh, sure," the stableman said hurriedly. "I didn't mean to poke my nose into your business none; I just sorta mentioned it because I know you and him rode in here together."

Almost before the liveryman had finished speaking, Ki came through the stable door. "Jessie!" he said. "And Nate, too. I didn't think you were coming back to town this evening."

"Nate needed a doctor," Jessie replied. She nodded almost imperceptibly toward the liveryman as she added, "We can talk about what happened while we're on the way to the cabin."

"Of course," Ki nodded. "I have some news for you, too."

After they'd left the stable and gotten beyond the lights of the last houses on the trail to Nate's cabin, Jessie told Nate, "You can follow the trail in the dark a lot better than we can. Do you feel up to leading the way?"

"Why, sure, Jessie. I know you wanta hear what all Ki's found out. And it ain't all that far. We'll be home in a half hour or less."

Turning to Ki, Jessie went on, "Unless you're too curious about Nate's bandage to wait, I'd like to know what you found out at the gambling house, Ki."

"More than I expected to," he replied. "And even if I'm curious, we can talk later about what happened to you and Nate. Just as we suspected, the gambling house is a cartel operation, Jessie. But before we start talking about the cartel, there's something else I've got to tell you."

"Something not connected with the cartel?" Jessie said. "It must be very important."

"Yes, it is," Ki nodded. "There's a woman going around the Mother Lode buying small placer claims from prospectors. And she's traveling under the name of Jessie Starbuck."

For a moment, Jessie was speechless. Then she asked Ki, "Do you know who she really is?"

"No, I don't really know anything except that apparently she's been buying claims in your name and posing as you for quite some time."

Jessie turned to Nate and asked, "Have you ever heard about her, Nate?"

"Not a word, Jessie," the old prospector replied. "She sure ain't bought no claims around here."

"Do you have a description of this woman, Ki?" Jessie asked. "Or know anything else about her?"

"I'm afraid not," he answered. "And I didn't want to show too much interest. I'd already found out enough to be convinced that the gambling house is a cartel operation."

"You found out about her from one of their people, then?" Jessie's voice held a frown, though her face was invisible in the darkness.

"Yes," Ki told her. "A woman who's—well, I suppose the best description of her would be one of their straw bosses. She knows a good deal about just one branch of their operation, but nothing important about the really important ones."

Jessie was too wise to probe further into the source of Ki's information or the methods he'd used to garner it.

Shifting the conversation back to its principal topic, she asked, "And she didn't know anything about me?"

Ki shook his head, then suddenly aware that Jessie couldn't see him in the dense blackness, said, "I'm sure the woman who told me about the imposter didn't have any idea that I'd even recognize your name. I was afraid to try to press her for more information. If I had, she might have gotten suspicious and stopped talking."

"Yes, I can understand that," Jessie said thoughtfully. "So you don't know anything about this woman who's impersonating me or where she might be now?"

"Only that she's somewhere in the south part of the Mother Lode, in the Calaveras country."

"But you don't know if she's still there?"

"No. I suppose she's still traveling from place to place, buying up small claims," Ki said.

Jessie went on, talking as much to herself as to Ki, "From what Frank Allison told me in San Francisco, she must know enough about California's land and water laws to understand that the cartel will need some kind of legal title to the little headwater creeks to operate those big dredges they're building."

"That thought occurred to me," Ki said when Jessie fell silent. "They'll have to own or lease mineral rights or hold title to the land itself."

"This fake Jessie Starbuck can't know much about the way the cartel operates, then," Jessie said thoughtfully. "When or if they want those claims she's bought, I'm sure they'll kill her and just steal the claim titles."

"Yes," Ki agreed. "I thought of that, too."

Nate broke into their conversation to say, "The cabin's just ahead, Jessie. Maybe you and Ki'll be a mite more comfortable talking when we get inside, build a fire, and get a pot of coffee going."

"You're right," Jessie agreed. "I didn't realize how nippy

108

the night air's gotten just in the past few minutes."

A half hour later, the horses had been hitched for the night and the cabin was growing warm from the blaze dancing in the fireplace. Jessie, Ki, and Nate were sitting at the table with cups of steaming coffee in front of them.

Turning to the old prospector, Jessie said, "It's been such a long time since I've even thought about the Mother Lode country that I've forgotten my geography. Just how big is it?"

"Well, it's a pretty good-size chunk of country, Jessie," he replied. "Us prospectors always figure the Mother Lode starts just a little ways north of here, up along the Yuba River, and runs south all the way down the foothills as far as Mariposa and Mormon Bar."

"How far is that in miles, Nate?" Ki asked.

"Right at a hundred and fifty, Ki," Nate said after a moment's concentration. "And give or take a little bit, it's maybe thirty miles wide most of the way."

"You've been over most of it, haven't you, Nate?" Jessie asked.

"There ain't much of it I've missed, Jessie. Course, I ain't been up to doing a lot of traveling of late; I just ain't spry enough. It ain't like when I first begun prospecting. In them days it wouldn't faze me a mite to load up my burro and push day and night for three or four days to get forty or fifty miles to where I'd heard somebody had hit good fresh color."

"And I'm sure nobody has any real idea how many little brooks and streams there are with placer claims along them?"

"Lord, no!" Nate exclaimed. "Why, there were thousands and thousands of us working them cricks before the rush petered out. Most of the Johnny-come-latelies gave up and scuttered back East or wherever they came from if they didn't make a strike quick enough. There's still enough of us real miners to keep things lively, though."

109

"It's hard for me to imagine what the Gold Rush was like," Jessie went on. "All the movement, all the thousands of men strung out along the streams panning for gold or digging into the hills looking for a vein."

"Oh, it was more'n a mite busy," Nate nodded. "But things was different, then, Jessie. There wasn't all this fol-derol and foofaraw about proving a claim afore you filed on it. All a man had to do then was write out his boundaries on a piece of paper and nail it to a tree someplace on his claim."

"There wasn't any legal record of it anywhere else?" Ki asked.

Nate shook his head. "Nope. That piece of paper was all."

"Then what protected your right if somebody else filed on the same piece of land?" Jessie asked.

"You done it yourself, Jessie. A man taken care of claim jumpers with a six-gun or rifle or shotgun. And he didn't get in trouble with no law for doing it, neither."

"Even before you filed on it formally?"

"Oh, sure. When the Rush was on, nobody'd ever file in town till they'd proved out their claim."

"I suppose there were a lot of claims filed on land that didn't have any gold deposits?" she went on.

"Sure. Only, if the claim didn't prove out, you'd jest walk away from it. There's plenty of claims that was filed on that never did pan out more'n an ounce or so."

Turning to Ki, Jessie said, "I think we've got a real job ahead of us, Ki."

"I'm sure we have," he nodded.

"But I guess we'll have to go down to the Calaveras country and make a start," Jessie went on. She turned to Nate. "You do know the land down there, don't you?"

"I used to, Jessie," Nate replied. "Course, it'll be a mite different now from when I seen it last. But I expect I can

110

still find my way around down there."

"And you don't mind leaving here for a little while?"

"Not a bit. I'd imagine everything'll still be here when we get back," Nate said.

"Good," Jessie nodded. "We'll get everything shipshape the first thing in the morning and start as soon as we can."

By midmorning the job of getting ready to leave was almost completed. Three sets of bulging saddlebags lay beside the cabin door; Jessie and Ki were waiting for Nate to come out after he'd finished barring the windows. The old miner stepped out of the cabin holding a heavy padlock and snapped it around the latch, then turned to them.

"I guess we're as ready as we'll ever be," he announced. "We might as well move out."

Nate bent to pick up his saddlebags and as he swung them to his shoulder his weather-beaten face paled and he gave a gasp of pain which he tried to smother unsuccessfully. Letting the saddlebags drop to the ground, he sagged against the cabin door.

"What's wrong?" Jessie asked. "Don't you feel well?"

"I'm all right, Jessie," Nate replied. "I got a twitch from a little hurt around where the doc took out that bullet."

"Has it bothered you before?" Jessie asked.

"Nothing aside from itching now and then."

Jessie said, "I'd better have a look at that wound."

"Now, I told you I'm all right, Jessie," Nate said gruffly. "I'm just fine. Let's mount up and start."

"If that wound's bothering you," Ki put in, "we'd better stop in Rough and Ready and see what the doctor says about it."

"I don't need no more doctoring, Ki," the old man answered quickly. "Anyway, the doc said it wasn't but a scratch."

They started on the trail, but before they were halfway

111

to town Nate was sagging in his saddle, his face flushed.

"I'm not going to listen to any argument," Jessie told the old miner. "We're stopping at Dr. Perry's office."

By the time they reined in at the doctor's office, Nate was swaying from side to side in his saddle. When the doctor pulled the shirt away from the wound, a glance at Nate's inflamed armpit and side told its own story, not only to the doctor, but to Jessie and Ki as well.

"Infection," Perry said. "It's going to need several days of treatment if you want to stay alive."

"Ain't there something you can do to fix it up quick, so's I can go with Jessie and Ki?" Nate asked.

Perry shook his head. "You'll need flax seed poultices that I'll have to change twice a day and every time they're changed the wound will have to be painted with carbolic. Besides that, purge you with extract of collocynth. You can't be taken care of while you're traveling."

"Do as Dr. Perry tells you, Nate," Jessie said. "Don't worry about me and Ki. We'll manage until you can recover and come join us."

"But you don't know the Calaveras country, Jessie!" Nate objected. "And I don't know of nobody—" he stopped short and after a moment's thought, went on, "Now, hold on! Maybe I do. Jessie, there's a young fellow I know that's just come back to town here. His name's Tim Moran, and him and me prospected together a year or so till he went south to the Calaveras diggings. How'd it be if I got him to go along with you?"

Jessie frowned and said hesitantly, "Well, if you know him and the two of you prospected together, I'm sure he'd be all right, Nate. But I'd have to meet him and talk with him before saying yes or no."

"It ought not to be hard to find him," Nate went on. "I ran into him less'n a week ago. He said he'd be staying at the hotel for a while, till he figured out where he'd go next.

112

Maybe Ki could go dig him up?"

Jessie and Ki had a silent consultation, and when Ki nodded, Jessie said, "All right. But if we can't find him in an hour or so, Ki and I will go on and you can join us later."

Ki returned with Tim Moran in less than the hour Jessie had allotted. From Moran's appearance, Jessie judged him to be in his middle thirties. A thatch of dark auburn hair sprang up when he raised his hat after being introduced to Jessie; Moran had the blue eyes and fair sun-reddened skin that matched his Irish name. He wore miner's denims—faded and patched, but scrupulously clean—and boots. When Nate introduced him to Jessie, his jaw dropped and he stared at her with a puzzled frown.

"Is something wrong?" Jessie asked.

"No, ma'am," Moran said slowly. "But maybe I'm kind of mixed up."

Turning to Ki, she asked, "Didn't you tell Mr. Moran what Nate had in mind?"

Ki shook his head. "No. I thought it'd be better if Nate did all the explaining. All I told him was that Nate had a job for him that he wanted to talk about."

"That's what's got me mixed up," Moran said quickly. "You see, I sold my claim to a lady named Jessie Starbuck, and you sure don't look nothing like her."

Chapter 11

For a moment, Jessie and Ki stared at Moran in silence. At last Jessie said, "I assure you, I'm not related to the lady who bought your claim, Mr. Moran. Whoever she is, I suspect she might be using the Starbuck name because before his death my father was well-known here in California."

"You're looking at the real Jessie Starbuck now, Tim," Nate put in. "I give you my word and bond on that. But how come you never told me about who you sold out to?"

"I—" Moran hesitated for a moment, then went on, "I guess it was because I was ashamed to, Nate. A man doesn't like to admit he's a fool, and that Jessie Starbuck who bought my claim down in the Calaveras diggings sure made me feel like a fool when she cheated me."

"Do you mind telling us how she cheated you?" Jessie asked.

"Well—" Moran hesitated again, then said, "I guess I'm not the only one she took in. You see, besides offering a good price, she had a lot of recommendations."

"Excuse me," Ki broke in when Moran stopped again. "Who had given her these recommendations?"

"Why, she had all kinds of letters from lawyers and so on, telling what a good head she had for business matters, and from bank presidents all up and down the Mother Lode that said she had money in their banks."

"And did you write to any of the men who'd signed the

letters she showed you?" Ki asked.

"Not till after I'd sold out to her," Moran replied. "The three or four I talked to later said they didn't write them. But on top of that, she was a pretty slick talker herself and paid me off with a bank draft. I didn't worry about taking it; just signed the claim over to her. Only the draft turned out not to be any good."

"And you couldn't get your claim back?" Jessie asked.

"I haven't yet, Miss Starbuck. I've gone to law about it, trying to get my title restored to me, but I guess you know going to law's not fast or easy."

Jessie nodded. "I understand quite well." She made up her mind quickly and added, "Perhaps you can help us find this woman, Mr. Moran. That's why we're going south. And I'll be glad to pay you a—"

"Hold on, Miss Starbuck," Moran broke in. "I don't mean to interrupt you, but I've got a score to settle with that woman myself. I'm as eager to find her as you are, and I'd feel like I was cheating you if I took pay for going along."

"I can't let you put in your time on my behalf without paying you," Jessie protested. "And I know it takes time to get back on your feet after you've been robbed."

"Well, I'll admit I'm not exactly flush," Moran said. "But I'd feel like I was taking unfair advantage of you if I let you pay me."

Jessie studied the problem for a moment, then said, "I'll make you an offer that I think is fair to both of us, Mr. Moran. I won't pay you wages, but I will pay all your expenses until we find her or both of us agree there's no use in looking further. Beyond that, I have lawyers on retainer in San Francisco, and I'll have them handle any kind of legal problems you might run into while trying to get back the title to your claim."

Moran smiled. "I can agree to that, Miss Starbuck. The

115

way you put it, I won't feel beholden, like I would if I was a hired hand. And you can depend on it, I'll do my level best to help you."

"You won't be making no mistake, Tim," Nate said. "Jessie is just like her pa was, and he was a man you could tie to."

Ki broke in before Nate could go on. "I think you've just make a good deal, Jessie. Now, I don't want to appear too eager, but if we're ever going to get to the Calaveras country we'd better think about starting."

"You're right," she agreed. "How long will it take you to get ready, Mr. Moran?"

"I've been staying in a hotel room and my horse is at the livery stable," Moran said. "The liveryman can have the horse saddled in about five minutes, and by that time I'll be through packing my saddlebags. Give me ten minutes, and we can be on our way." Then he added, "It won't be a minute too soon, either. I've been rankling for a long time about being a fool, and this is the best chance I'll have to get back what belongs to me."

Tim Moran reined in at the crest of a low bluff overlooking a wide, level valley and gestured toward the town below. He said to Jessie and Ki, "I guess Columbia's the best place we'll find to stay. It's got a new hotel, and that's more than you can say for the rest of the towns around here."

Jessie and Ki looked down at the town. In the slanting rays of the late afternoon sun, its center formed a tidy geometric pattern of red brick buildings. The town's core was surrounded by a sprawl of small dwellings in which neatly painted houses mingled in a hodgepodge with log cabins and tumbledown shacks. A creek wound through the town, zigzagging from the low, jagged walls of ocher soil at the eastern end of the broad, shallow valley in which Columbia lay.

"It looks like a nice enough town," Ki observed.

"Oh, it's better than a lot of Mother Lode towns," Moran said. "I understand there was a lot of talk about making Columbia the state capitol a while back, but it lost out to Sacramento. Anyhow, everybody got excited and begun building those brick buildings when the capitol fever took hold."

"Where is your claim, Tim?" Jessie asked.

"It's in the next valley, Jessie," Moran replied, pointing to the eastern wall. "You see where the break is. A stream cuts through it and the gap opens into a valley half again as big as this one. My claim's about in the middle of it."

"It's not far, then," Jessie went on. "Would you like to ride over and see it before we go into town?"

"Well, even if it's not rightly my claim any longer, I admit I'm curious to see if that woman's put somebody to working it," Moran replied. "It's going on ten months now since I was here last, so if you're sure you don't mind—"

"Of course not," Jessie assured him. "As a matter of fact, I'm a little bit curious to see it myself."

"It doesn't look too far," Ki seconded. "There ought to be plenty of time for us to take a quick look and get to town before dark."

In contrast to the first hundred miles of their four-day journey from Rough and Ready, this day had been an easy one. Instead of swinging to the southwest where the foothills flattened out into the valleys of the Sacramento and San Joaquin Rivers, Moran had led them almost due south in as straight a line as possible. Over the back-country trails beaten by the forty-niners and their successors, they'd traveled through the stumps and growth covering the high foothills that rose to the base of the towering Sierra Nevada.

They'd passed through the dying gold camps of Dutch Flat, Iowa Hill, Michigan Bluff, crossed Smith Flat and Grizzly Flats, and then slanted to the southwest. When they

117

reached the main Gold Rush trail at Fiddletown, the going was much easier. Here, prospecting and mining were still the residents's way of life. There was no growth on the rolling hills, just mile after mile of low-crested chamisa and redbud between long stretches of barren ground. The creeks still ran brown from the claims upstream which had become active mines producing gold ore in paying amounts from the sluices.

Stagecoaches ran on the main trail, and the towns through which they passed were still alive. In contrast to most of the places they'd seen farther north, many of the towns settled during the Gold Rush were almost bustling: Jackson and Mokolumne Hill and Angel's Camp.

At the forks of the Stanislaus River, a mule-powered ferry had taken them across the stream, and they'd followed the river for a short distance before cutting due south to the rim of the red dirt valley where they'd now reined in.

Their trip had accomplished more than their just covering the miles to their destination. By the middle of the second day, Moran had changed from an unknown stranger into a compatible companion to Jessie and Ki, and they'd abandoned formality. He led the way now along the vestigial trail that ran at the rim of the bluff, and Jessie and Ki spent more time gazing into the wide valley as they passed by than they did trying to watch the trail in front of them.

They'd covered perhaps two miles along the rim, and Columbia looked like a toy town with its red brick core of buildings surrounded by scattered houses. Looking ahead, Jessie could see now that the shallow valley was shaped like an hourglass, and they were approaching its narrow waist.

Between them and the town the valley floor was covered with patchy low-growing vegetation, scattered clumps rising from the scant cover of short grass. Jessie had just turned in her saddle to say something to Ki when Moran reined in

118

so abruptly that she almost overran him.

"Is something wrong, Tim?" she asked, seeing him rise in his stirrups and stare ahead.

When young Moran made no reply, Jessie leaned forward and tried looking beyond him, but they had reached the point where the rim curved inward to form the waist of hourglass. It was a narrow curving spit of land with steep dropoffs on both sides, and because Moran's horse was squarely in the center, she could not see around his broad shoulders.

After a moment, Moran turned and shook his head. He said, "I just don't believe what I'm looking at."

Kneeing his horse to one side of the trail to make room, he gestured for Jessie to come up beside him. She toed her horse ahead and looked beyond Tim's pointing finger. Then Jessie gasped, a mixture of surprise and consternation. Hearing her exclamation, and seeing there was not room ahead for a third horse on the narrow spit, Ki dismounted and walked up to join his companions. He joined them in gazing at the scene, shaking his head as he stared.

For perhaps a half mile ahead the floor of the valley was level. Like the area behind them, the strip of ground just past the gap was dotted with small clumps of low-growing vegetation between expanses of short curling grass. The narrow line of growth ended abruptly, as though it had been slashed with a single stroke of a giant knife, and beyond the line of the slash lay devastation.

Nothing grew there. There was no soil, no earth to cover the surface of the wide embanked lines of pink and white rocks that stretched over the valley in a swathe perhaps two miles wide. The lines lay straight, as though they were fields that had been plowed into furrows, ready to be planted. The only sign of vegetation was an occasional gnarled root of a bush that rose like a black snake from the rock heaps. Some of the rocks were as big as a man's torso, and others scarcely larger than a fist. Here and there in the bottoms of some of the furrows small puddles of brown water stood, throwing back in sullen dullness the rays of the westward slanting sun.

"How terrible!" Jessie gasped. Then as the first shock of what she was looking at began to taper off, she went on, "The only thing that could've caused this is a gold dredge, Tim. But it'd have to be a very big one. I got a glimpse of a dredge or two a few years ago when Ki and I were traveling through Montana, and that's how the land behind them looked."

"Those were small dredges, Jessie," Ki remarked. "The one that did this damage must be a monster."

"However big it is, it sure tore up what used to be my claim," Tim commented. His lips were compressed angrily. "I guess that woman posing as Jessie Starbuck must've sold it right away."

"I'm sure she did," Jessie agreed. "The—" she stopped just in time to avoid mentioning the cartel and covered her pause by going on quickly, "The men who did this would have to be sure they had mineral rights to the whole valley before they started dredging."

"There were six of us working claims here," Tim frowned. "I guess the others sold theirs at the same time I did." Still looking at the ruined valley, he went on, "It was real nice here when I first came prospecting it. Four or five little brooks that ran into the creeks, green brush, now and again a deer wandering by. But the placer poachers have sure ruined it now."

They fell silent again, looking at the devastated land. In all of the area they could see, nothing moved, but after Jessie had recovered from her first wave of shocked surprise, she heard in the distance from the head of the valley the faint chugging of a steam engine and a continuing low, rumbling, clashing noise. Beyond the winnowed rocks something moved into view, and all three fixed their eyes on it.

Advancing at a snaillike pace was what appeared to be a cabin or house mounted on a flat barge. It inched across the valley floor. Puffs of white smoke jutted now and then from a chimney that rose above the cabin. A boom or slanted mast protruded behind it, and they could see a steady discharge of water mixed with stones dropping from its peak. As its painfully slow advance continued they saw forming behind it a row of rocks that matched the stone winnows that covered the valley floor.

"Why, that's the gold dredge!" Jessie exclaimed.

"It sure as hell is," Tim replied. "Excuse my swearing, Jessie, but when I look at what the placer pirates are doing here, I get mad enough to chew nails."

"It's sad, all right," Ki agreed. "This land will be useless now for a long time."

"At least little prospectors like me don't do any damage," Tim went on. "Some folks don't like us because we mess up the edges of a creek or a river, but at least we don't ruin it forever. Why, it'll be a hundred years before anything will grow on the land those dredges are working!"

"Tim," Jessie asked, frowning, "when you were working your claim up here, did you hear any talk about dredging?"

"Oh, sure," he said. "But I didn't pay much attention to it, Jessie. There's always a lot of chatter and gossip and wild talk going around in mining country. Why?"

"Because it takes quite a bit of time to build a dredge as big as the one up the valley there," she frowned. "And it must have been built, or at least assembled, somewhere close by."

"I'd imagine that the materials were brought in quietly, a little at a time," Ki suggested. "They'd need a small engine, a steam boiler, and the buckets and lumber, but none of those things is too uncommon in mining country."

"That's right," Tim agreed. "There was always some kind of equipment being hauled past my claim, big freight wagons and now and then a mule train."

"That dredge must be about the size of the two that those Chinese coolies are building on the Yuba River, up by Rough and Ready," Ki said thoughtfully. "I didn't have time to go look at the place where they're working, but I'm sure they'd be using the same set of plans."

"You're probably right," Jessie nodded. "And we don't have any way of knowing how many others they're getting ready."

"We can't cover all the streams in the foothills, Jessie," Ki said. "But I'm sure all we've seen so far is just the tip of the iceberg."

"You mean there's somebody having dredges built all up and down the Mother Lode?" Tim asked.

"Perhaps," Jessie told him. "Ki and I think so, but we can't be certain yet. We don't have enough information."

"Then that woman who's using your name might be connected with whoever's building the dredges," Tim went on, a thoughtful frown forming on his face. "She could be buying up claims they need to get enough places to operate big dredges."

"Yes, that's a possibility," Jessie agreed. "But that's something we can talk about later, Tim. Right now, there's nothing we can do about the dredge. I think we'd better go to Columbia and find a hotel and restaurant. We can talk tonight about what our next move should be."

Silent and depressed by what they'd seen, the trio rode slowly back to town. Dusk was settling by the time they reached Columbia, and the streets were crowded with men. Most of them wore the rough clothing favored by miners and prospectors, and it was obvious that they'd come into town from claims they were working in the vicinity. Jessie, Ki, and Tim found rooms at Fallon's Hotel and had dinner

122

in the hotel's crowded dining room. After they'd finished eating, Jessie looked around at the busy, noisy tables.

"We certainly can't talk privately here," she said. "And I'm not sure we'd be wise to try to make any plans tonight. All of us are so tired from our trip that we might not be able to see the forest for the trees."

"That makes sense," Ki agreed. "We'll all be able to think more clearly in the morning."

"It suits me," Moran nodded. "I guess I'm a little more used to roughing it than you two are because I'm not all that tired yet. I think I'll walk around town and see if I can't run into some of the men I know who're still working claims in the neighborhood. Maybe I can pick up a little useful gossip."

"We'll meet at breakfast, then," Jessie said, standing up. "Right now, all I can think of is soaking in a tub of hot water for a few minutes and getting into bed."

Ki woke with his usual quickness, fully alert, when the light tapping sounded on the door of his room. Stopping only long enough to step into his loose trousers and strap the case holding his *shuriken* on his left forearm, he padded barefoot to the door and opened it a crack. When he peered out he saw Tim Moran standing in the dim nightlight that illuminated the hall.

"What's wrong, Tim?" he asked, opening the door to let the young prospector enter.

"I didn't want to knock on Jessie's door," Tim said. "But I figured you'd know whether she'd want to be told."

"Told what?"

"Some news I picked up at the Miner's Rest Saloon a few minutes ago. I ran into one of my old friends, a fellow who worked the claim next to mine when I was here before."

"If you think it's important, I'm sure Jessie would want to know," Ki told him. "But perhaps you'd better tell me first; I'll know then whether or not we should wake her."

"Oh, it's important, all right," Tim said. "A bunch of the miners who're working little claims up along the south fork of the Stanislaus are as mad as everybody else is about that gold dredge working the upper valley. They're going to blow it up tonight."

Ki's quick mind was exploring the consequences of such an act almost before Moran finished speaking. As soon as the cartel bosses in San Francisco got news of the bombing, they would send men to the Mother Lode to investigate it and take revenge on the miners who had set off the explosive. Almost certainly they would place some important cartel member in charge of such an important job; perhaps even one of the bosses himself would take charge.

Ki was well aware of the efficiency with which the cartel operated. In a place as small as Columbia, they would soon learn that he and Jessie were there. In all probability, the cartel would jump to the conclusion that Jessie had somehow been involved in destroying the dredge. The result would almost certainly be an immediate and open attack on them.

Reaching for his jacket, Ki told Moran, "I'm sure Jessie will want to know of this. I'll go with you to wake her."

Almost before Ki finished speaking, the floor shivered and quaked for several seconds and before its quivering ended the muffled boom of a distant explosion reached his ears.

"They've done it!" Tim exclaimed.

"Yes," Ki replied. "And I don't think we need to worry now about waking Jessie. Come on, Tim. Let's go tell her what's happened."

124

Chapter 12

"Blown up the gold dredge!" Jessie exclaimed after Ki and Tim explained the source of the blast that had awakened her.

"They already had the blasting powder planted by the time I heard what they were going to do," Tim explained. "I hurried back so you'd know what was going on, but they touched it off while Ki and I were talking."

Like Ki, Jessie had begun calculating the aftermath of the blast while Tim was still explaining. She looked at Ki, who was waiting just inside the door, and asked, "I suppose you're thinking the same thing I am?"

Ki nodded. "I'm sure I am. Both of us know how their minds work, Jessie. As soon as the news about the dredge gets to San Francisco, they'll start concentrating their forces here. They can't afford to accept a major setback without making somebody pay for it."

"Yes. If they don't go out for revenge their prestige would drop to zero," Jessie agreed. "Luckily for us, Columbia's far enough off the beaten track to be hard to reach. They'll need time to get here, so we don't have to hurry planning our move."

Ki replied as though he were thinking aloud. "If they send men from San Francisco, they'll have to go to Stockton by train and travel here to Columbia on the stagecoach or horseback. I'd say we can stay one more day without worrying."

"I doubt that they'll wait for anyone from San Francisco to get here," Jessie said. "They'll send someone from there, of course, because they'll want men here with more authority than those already in Columbia."

"They're sure to have a key man in Stockton," Ki nodded. "And that's not quite sixty miles. I'd say we ought to get out of here sooner than we intended."

"You're right," Jessie nodded. "But we're not ready to make our own move, Ki. We can't let this dredging business divert us from what we started to do."

"It seemed important at the time," Ki reminded her.

"Yes, and it's just as important now. But there's a lot of ground remaining to be covered, and when you mentioned Stockton it reminded me that I've still got to talk to those farmers who're leasing land in the valleys."

"This would be a good time," Ki agreed. "We should be able to work there without worrying while their attention's concentrated on Columbia."

During the rapid exchange between Jessie and Ki, Tim Moran had been looking from one to the other, a puzzled frown deepening on his face. Now he said, "I don't mean to be nosy, Jessie, but will you please tell me what you and Ki are saying? Who's the 'they' you're talking about?"

"It would take too long to tell you the whole story, Tim," Jessie answered. "Please, just take my word that we're reasonably sure we know who that gold dredge belonged to and that we have good reasons for wanting to leave Columbia right away."

"You mean it's somebody who's got a grudge against you?"

"I suppose that's the simplest way to put it," Jessie said. "A very old and bitter grudge."

"Well, I'm not trying to poke into your business, Jessie,

126

but why don't you just stay here and fight it out with whoever it is?" Moran asked.

"There's a time to fight and a time to wait for a better chance to win," Jessie replied. "And this is a time to wait." She saw that the young prospector was still puzzled and went on, "I'm not trying to evade your questions, Tim. It's just something I can't talk about."

"It sounds to me like you're up against some kind of a gang," Moran frowned.

"You could put it that way," Ki agreed.

"You think the woman who called herself Jessie Starbuck is tied to them somehow?" Moran went on.

"It's quite likely," Jessie said. "And just because we're leaving Columbia now doesn't mean we're going to give up looking for her. I'd like for you to stay with us, and I'm sure Ki would, too."

"Of course, I would," Ki said quickly.

"There's not much I can do around here by myself," Tim said thoughtfully. "As long as you keep looking for that woman who cheated me, I'm going to stick with you both."

"Good," Jessie nodded. She turned to Ki again. "How soon should we try to leave?"

"Noon tomorrow ought to be plenty of time," Ki said. "If Tim works fast, he should be able to cover a good bit of ground in the morning. That explosion could be heard for a long way, Jessie. It's going to bring a lot of miners and prospectors out of the hills and into Columbia."

"Now, that hadn't occurred to me before, Ki," Moran said. "It stands to reason, though." He thought for a moment, then added, "I'll bet there's a lot of 'em already on the road here."

"And I imagine the ones who live in town are packed into the saloons by now," Ki went on.

"Sure they are!" Tim exclaimed. "And talking their heads off about who could've done it."

"Talk creates more talk," Ki observed quietly. "We won't be the only ones who'll connect that explosion with the woman who bought up all the claims in the area where that gold dredge was working."

"You're right about that, too, Ki," Moran nodded. "But instead of waiting for morning, how would it be if I move around the saloons for the rest of the night? I know a lot of those fellows. They won't hold anything back from me."

Having set out to bring exactly that reaction from Tim, Ki remained silent and signaled Jessie with his eyes.

Jessie responded to Ki's unspoken signal. She said to Moran, "That's a good idea, Tim. You do that, and as soon as the bank opens in the morning I'll see if my impersonator left a trail there. Ki can be getting our gear ready while you and I are asking questions. We'll have lunch early and compare notes while we're traveling."

"We'll make better time tomorrow," Tim Moran told Jessie and Ki as they rode through the gathering dusk toward the twinkling lights ahead that told them they were close to Angels Camp. "There's a pretty good road from here on into Stockton."

"I don't think we've done too badly today," Jessie said. "Even if we didn't leave Columbia with a great deal of information, we do have a pattern forming that ought to help us close in on that woman who claims to be me."

"We're a lot further ahead than when we started," Ki reminded Moran. "At least we're reasonably sure that she came back to this area less than a month ago. That beats the trail we started on, Tim. It was almost a year ago that she swindled you."

They rode on in silence. The road was straighter now, and it widened as they passed the twinkling lights in the windows of the houses and cabins that steadily crowded closer together as they approached the town. In contrast to the excited groups of men who'd been moving through the streets when they left Columbia, Angels Camp was quiet. There were people on the streets and in the saloons, but no hint of excitement was in the air.

Angels Camp was a town of small, shabby buildings. Its residents seemed to have lost heart when the lodes nearby were exhausted in the early years of the Gold Rush and the prospectors passed it by, heading for the rich new strikes at Columbia and Mokolumne Hill, Jackson, and Eldorado. A freshly painted, white-columned, two-story building ahead stood out like a beacon, as did the sign HOTEL on the facade above the columns.

Jessie turned to Tim and asked, "Do you know which of the hotels here is our best choice?"

"I'm afraid I don't know much about Angels Camp, Jessie," he replied. "When I was in Columbia, I never did have any real need to stop; all I ever did was pass through here on my way to Stockton or San Francisco."

"We'll just take our chances with that one ahead, then," she said. "We might not have a choice; I haven't seen any other hotel signs. At least we'd better stop and see what this one's like."

She turned her horse to the rail. Ki and Tim followed her example. All three dismounted and went inside. The lobby was small and spartanly furnished, and Jessie noticed that the hotel had neither a bar nor a dining room. The carpet showed signs of wear, and the paneled pine walls were in need of a fresh coat of varnish, but the place looked clean. As they reached the reception desk a young man came from a door behind the desk and stood waiting.

"Welcome to the Casa de Oro," he said. Though he spoke without an accent, it was clear from his intonation and appearance that he was of Spanish descent. He went on, "You wish rooms, of course." It was a statement rather than a question. "How many rooms, please?"

"Three," Jessie replied.

"We will be happy to accommodate you," he smiled, opening the well-worn, leather-bound register and handing Jessie a pen.

When Jessie glanced at the book she could see at once that the hotel had few patrons. The dates opposite the signatures were usually several days apart and the page was only three-quarters filled. She took the pen and as she ran her eyes down the page, looking for the first blank line, one of the names near the top seemed to jump out and command her attention. Written in a sprawling loosely formed script, the name was her own.

Placing her finger beside the name, Jessie turned to show the ledger to Ki and Tim, but before either of them could comment she said in a low voice, "Let's don't confuse the clerk by all of us talking at once. I'll see what I can find out from him." Turning back to the desk, she turned the ledger to allow the clerk to read it, pointed to the fake signature, and asked, "Do you remember this lady?"

"Miss Starbuck?" he asked. "But of course. Her family name is well-known in the Mother Lode. As you see, she was our guest for three days. She is a friend of yours, or perhaps you are related?"

"No," Jessie said. "I've never seen her. But I'd like very much to find her. You see, my name is Starbuck. Jessie Starbuck."

"But this is not possible!" the clerk exclaimed. "You do not look at all alike!"

"There's no reason we should," Jessie said sharply. "We're not related, I assure you. The woman who signed your register is using my name illegally. She's not only impersonating me, but she's also swindling miners and prospectors, buying their claims, and paying for them with forged bank drafts."

"But those are criminal acts!" the clerk protested. "And she was such a nice lady! So polite, so generous!"

"I'm sure she could afford to be generous, since she was spending stolen money," Jessie said. "I'm trying to find her and stop her from using my name. I'd like for you to tell me everything you remember about her that might help me find her."

"I beg your pardon, *señorita,*" the clerk said, his voice calmer now as he recovered from his first surprise. "But how do I know that you are—" he stopped, frowning, as he searched for words—"You will forgive me for asking, but how can I be sure that the Miss Starbuck who stayed here is not the real one, and you the imposter?"

Jessie saw the logic of the man's question. She nodded and said, "Unfortunately, you can't. And I'm sure you wouldn't take the word of my companions as identification; they'd quite naturally back up my story."

"Yes, that is true," the clerk agreed. A thoughtful frown wrinkled his brow and he went on, "But you have stopped here to visit friends, perhaps? Someone in town who is known to me and to you, and can assure me that you are who you claim to be?"

"As far as I know, there's nobody in Angels Camp who knows me," Jessie frowned.

"Aha!" the clerk exclaimed. "Now you make me doubt your story even more! The other Miss Starbuck had a family friend here, a man well-known to me."

"I'd like to talk to him, then," Jessie said quickly. "What's his name, and where can I find him?"

"You will have no trouble finding him," the clerk replied. "He is the owner of the Calaveras Bank. His name is Albert Standfield. He visited Miss Starbuck here in the hotel two or three times during her stay."

Jessie searched her memory quickly, then shook her head.

"I'm afraid I don't know the name. But if he claimed to know this woman who's impersonating me, I want to meet him."

In spite of Jessie's earlier request, Ki broke in to say quietly, "You do know Albert Standfield, Jessie, but it's no wonder you don't remember him. You haven't seen him since you were a small girl. Mr. Standfield was one of your father's good friends when Alex was beginning to expand the importing business during his early days in San Francisco."

"Thank you, Ki," Jessie said. She turned back to face the clerk. "I'm sure the bank's closed by now. Can you tell me where Mr. Standfield lives?"

"His home is a short distance from town, but you will not find him there," the clerk replied. "At this time of day, Mr. Standfield will be in Finney's Saloon, having a *copita* before he goes home to dinner."

"Would you like for me to go find him, Jessie?" Ki asked. "He might remember me; I was with Alex a number of times when he and Standfield were together."

"Please do, Ki," she nodded. "Tim and I will wait here."

"It is very close, Finney's Saloon," the clerk said. He gestured at the lobby. "If you would like to sit down while you are waiting—"

Jessie nodded and, with Tim following her, went to one of the well-worn divans and sat down. Tim asked, "Don't you think landing on this woman's trail so quick is going to help us find her, Jessie?"

"It certainly should, Tim. This is the first time we've gotten on her trail so soon. It might be just what we need to close in on her."

"I'd sure like nothing better. You know, if every miner she cheated like she did me got back the title to his claim, we might be able to get together and stop those placer pirates."

"And that would be a good thing," she agreed.

Tim went on, "I don't see how anybody could believe that woman was you, now that I've been around you for a few days. She didn't look like you or talk like you even a little bit."

"She was dealing with people who'd never seen me," Jessie reminded him. "It's just luck that we've run into someone who knew my father and who might remember me. Even though it's been a long time since Mr. Standfield has seen me, I'm sure I can convince him that I'm really who I say I am."

Ki returned before Jessie and Tim could say anything more. With him was an elderly man, a bit on the portly side, dressed more formally than the miners they'd seen on the street. Despite his age, his step was quick and his carriage erect. His eyes were bright blue and his florid face cleanly shaven. He set his gaze on Jessie the instant he saw her and hurried to where she and Tim were sitting.

"Mr. Standfield?" Jessie asked, rising to meet him and extending her hand. "I hope you remember me."

Standfield took her hand, but said nothing for a moment while he studied her face. At last he said, "Jessie Starbuck." Then he shook his head and went on. "Ki told me a little bit about the reason you're here. Looking at you now, I wonder how I could've been such a damned fool. Even if you were just a little girl the last time I saw you, there's a lot of Alex Starbuck in your face and voice."

"More than the woman who's been using my name has, I hope," Jessie said.

"I figured you'd changed," Standfield confessed. "And that woman passing herself off as you—well, let's save talking about her for later, Jessie. I've done you a real bad service, and I'm sorry. Let's sit down and talk, and you tell me what the devil's going on."

Tim had risen to his feet when Jessie stood up and now

133

he said, "I'll go check out the town with Ki, Jessie. You won't need us here."

As Jessie and Standfield settled down on the divan, the banker went on, "You know, if I'd listened to my instincts, I'd have investigated that woman before I accepted her as you."

"There wasn't any way you could've known," Jessie told him, "after so many years. And I'm sure she put up a convincing story or you wouldn't've accepted her."

"Oh, she was a good talker," the banker said. "And I was so tickled to see Alex Starbuck's daughter after all these years that I guess I didn't pay enough attention to things that might have tipped me off."

"Things? What kind of things, Mr. Standfield?"

"Now, you ought to know better than to 'mister' me," Standfield said. "What was it you used to call me when you were a little girl? If you recall, it was your father's idea."

Suddenly the name gushed from some deep fountain of Jessie's memory. She said, "Uncle Bert! Of course!"

"That's something the woman passing herself off as you didn't know," Standfield nodded. "And something else that ought to have waken me up. She knew about Ki, but said he was married and stayed behind with his family. Then, when I asked her about that ranch Alex bought when he moved from California to Texas, she called it the Circle S instead of the Circle Star. But I just figured I'd forgotten, or that after Alex had lived there a while he'd begun calling it the Circle S, too."

"You certainly can't be blamed for that, Uncle Bert," Jessie said. She was surprised that the nickname had remained buried in her memory for so many years and now came to her tongue quite naturally. "I couldn't've been more than five or six years old the last time we saw each other."

"No, and I didn't see your father for a long spell, Jessie.

134

After he moved to Texas and your mother died and all, we'd have a meal together once or twice a year when he'd come back to California on business. But when I bought this little bank here and moved away from The City, we didn't keep in touch as closely as we should have. As I recall, I didn't see him for about ten years before he was—" Standfield paused almost imperceptibly, caught himself, and went on, "—before he died."

"I've finally accepted the fact that Alex was murdered," Jessie said quietly. "But I still miss him. And I spend as much time as I can on the Circle Star because I love the ranch as much as he did. But it's been such a long time since we've seen each other that I can understand how this woman impersonating me could fool you. And I'm hoping you can help me track her down."

"You'd want to stop her, of course," the banker nodded. "And I think I might be able to help you, at least a little bit. Of course, I was pretty upset when I discovered that she was paying for the claims she bought with worthless drafts. I didn't find out about that until a few days ago because she was smart enough not to do any business with my bank."

"I need all the help I can get," Jessie told him. "And I didn't learn about her posing as me until a few days ago."

"That's what's brought you to the Mother Lode, I suppose?"

"In a roundabout way, yes. But that's a long story, and—"

Standfield broke in. "I've got an idea, Jessie. We need to have a long talk, not only about this business of somebody posing as you, but about what's happened all these years since we've seen each other. Now, I've got a big house just outside Angels Camp, and a cook that's got a big supper, twice what I can handle, waiting for me. I want you and

135

Ki and that young fellow who seems to be traveling with you to come out and have supper with me and stay the night."

"I can't impose on you that way, Uncle Bert!" Jessie protested. "Just appear out of a blue sky and—"

"Nonsense!" Standfield broke in. "There's plenty of room at the house for you and your friends and more than enough supper will be on the table when we get there."

"Well—" Jessie did not hesitate long. Though she knew that some of their talk would bring up sad memories for both of them, she accepted the invitation if only for the chance to talk with Alex's old friend. She went on, "I'll take your invitation with all my thanks, Uncle Bert."

"Good! And on the way to the house, I'll stop at the bank and pick up some papers—notices from the San Francisco Clearing-House about the worthless drafts this woman's spread around, things of that kind—that might help you track her down."

"Anything you have will help me," Jessie said. "I don't intend to stop until I've found her. She's misusing the Starbuck name, and I'm going to see that she goes to jail!"

Chapter 13

"I wish I hadn't been so quick to accept that lying woman's word that she was you, Jessie," Standfield said as the two sat at the table in his dining room after dinner.

Knowing Jessie as well as he did, Ki had seen that she wanted to talk privately with Albert Standfield, and soon after they'd eaten he suggested to Tim that they turn in early.

"If I'd just been a little more suspicious after she made those mistakes," the old banker went on, "I'd have—"

Jessie broke in to say, "Don't start blaming yourself again, Uncle Bert. I don't blame you. It's been such a long time since you saw me last, I can understand your mistake."

"It makes me angry just the same," the banker told her. "I should've known better than to believe her when she told me she was expanding the Starbuck interests into gold mining and trying to hold down the price of those placer claims by moving very quietly."

"Is that what she said?" Jessie asked.

"Yes, and she made me believe it for a while. Oh, she was a convincing liar, all right. I didn't really doubt her until I saw those notices in the confidential bulletin I got just the other day from the San Francisco Clearing-House."

"You mentioned that bulletin at the hotel," Jessie said. "I didn't quite understand what you were talking about, but that wasn't the time or place to ask you to explain it."

"We had a regular flood of bank swindlers here on the coast a number of years ago, Jessie," Standfield said, "so the banks in San Francisco set up a private detective force in connection with the Clearing-House. You understand about the Clearing-House, don't you?"

"I think so. It sorts out the drafts from banks outside San Francisco and distributes them to the banks that are responsible for paying them. Am I right?"

"Well, it's a little more complicated than that, but you boiled it right down to a nubbin," Standfield replied. "If you gave somebody a draft on your bank in Texas, and they cashed it here at my bank, we'd send the draft to the Clearing-House and they'd collect from the Texas bank and send my bank the payment when they got it."

"Doesn't that take a lot of extra work?" Jessie frowned.

"Of course, but in the long run it saves the banks a lot of time and helps us to catch swindlers faster. But as I was saying, when the bank frauds got bad a few years ago, the Clearing-House started issuing warning bulletins and organized its own detective force to try to cut down the swindling."

"And did it?"

"It worked well enough for us to keep it in operation," Standfield nodded. "But as you say, it's a bit slow. It wasn't until a few days ago that I saw the warning in the Clearing-House bulletin about the woman who's impersonating you."

"You mean that my name was listed as a swindler?" Jessie asked indignantly, her eyes flashing with anger.

"Now, hold on!" Standfield said quickly. "The bulletin doesn't list names at all. Since it's a private organization, if it erroneously published some innocent person's name as a swindler, the Clearing-House could be sued, and juries aren't usually very sympathetic toward banks when they make mistakes like that."

"I don't think I would be either," Jessie replied. "But go

on, Uncle Bert. Did you recognize the woman from what you read in the bulletin?"

Standfield shook his head. "I wasn't sure, but it started me wondering. I was going to write Walter Edmonds and ask him to find out for me, but I haven't had time yet."

"You might have had another surprise if you'd written. I visited Walter a few days ago. He was the one who warned me that the Starbuck farm leases in the San Joaquin Valley might be in danger."

"What kind of danger?" the banker asked.

"This woman who's using my name has been buying up placer claims with those worthless drafts, Uncle Bert. From what Ki and I have uncovered since we started trying to find her, she's acting for a group that intends to start operating gold dredges on a very big scale."

"Damned placer pirates!" Standfield exclaimed. "They're worse than the hydraulic miners were before Alex organized enough opposition to stop them! They've already ruined a lot of gold producing streams here in the Mother Lode, and I'd hate to see them move down into the valleys."

"So would I," Jessie nodded.

"That explains something I haven't been able to figure out until now," Standfield went on. "I couldn't see why anybody'd be interested in buying small placer claims. Usually when a prospector hits a good stretch of paydirt, he works it himself until the ore peters out and then starts prospecting for another claim."

"But from the little I know about placer mining, panning a claim never gets all the gold out," Jessie replied. "I understand that a gold dredge can operate profitably if there's only ten or fifteen cents worth of raw gold in every ton of dirt it brings up from the bottom. Of course, nothing will grow on dredged land for a hundred years, and the dredges kill the little tributary streams, so the rivers die, too."

"Yes, that's true," Standfield nodded. "But aside from

139

stopping this woman from impersonating you, what's your interest in gold dredging?"

"I'm out to stop it, Uncle Bert," Jessie said, her voice showing her firm determination. "You must have known that Alex bought a lot of very valuable, irrigated farmland down in San Joaquin Valley."

"Of course. I worked with him on some of the purchases, but you'd have been too young to remember things of the kind. As I recall, though, Alex wasn't very interested in farming."

"He was interested in people, Uncle Bert. Before he died he began leasing that land to farmers who'd proved they were good workers, but couldn't save enough money to buy land of their own. I've been carrying on what he started, and I want to continue leasing, just as I feel he'd expect me to."

"And because gold dredges kill the little creeks and brooks of the tributaries, they'll eventually kill the rivers," the old banker said, thinking aloud. "You don't want to see good farmland become worthless because it has no water."

"And I don't want good farmers to be forced to give up land that can produce food," Jessie added.

"Then the woman impersonating you is just an agent, what crooks would call a front, for the gold dredge operators." Standfield sat silent for a moment, frowning, then he said, "Correct me if I'm wrong, Jessie, but somehow I get the idea that you believe this woman impersonating you isn't acting just for herself."

"You're right," Jessie nodded. "From what Ki and I discovered in the Yuba River country, Alex's old enemies are behind this whole scheme."

Standfield's eyebrows shot up. "The cartel?"

Jessie nodded. "You're one of the few men who was in Alex's complete confidence, Uncle Bert. You and Ki are the only ones I can really talk with about the cartel."

"I'm too old to be much help to you, though, Jessie," the banker said, regret in his voice. "I was a lot younger when I worked with your father."

"There's not much that I can do until we pick up a trail that'll lead us to whoever's behind the dredging scheme," Jessie said. "The woman posing as me is the only lead Ki and I have, and that's pretty much at a dead end right now."

"Wait a minute!" Standfield exclaimed. "Maybe I can help you at that!"

"How?"

"Those Clearing-House bulletins. They give the names of the banks that got the faked drafts and the dates the drafts were put through by the people who took them. If you're not too tired, just sit here for a little while and let me see what I can figure out from this file of bulletins I brought home."

While Jessie waited, Albert Standfield began going through the Clearing-House bulletins, listing bank locations and dates. His years of banking experience paid off. After an hour's patient work, he handed Jessie a rough chart that traced the imposter's path through a long series of swindles.

"Do you notice the same thing I do?" Standfield asked after he'd spread the finished chart on the table and explained it to Jessie.

"About all I notice is that my impersonator has been very busy," she replied. "She's certainly covered a lot of ground. But what do you see that I've missed, Uncle Bert?"

"That woman you're after hasn't used any San Francisco bank on her fake drafts. And there's another Bay town she's avoided. Stockton. Since it's right close to the Mother Lode, I'd venture a guess that she's making her headquarters there, and she's smart enough not to stir up any trouble in her home territory."

"You're suggesting we head for Stockton?" Jessie asked.

"It'd make sense to me," the old banker replied, "because

in order for her to operate, her bosses must provide her with money—quite a bit of money, since not all the miners she buys out will take a bank draft."

"And they'd get the money to her through a bank?" Jessie inquired. "How could they do that without giving away their own identity?"

"From what I recall of the days Alex and I worked together, they'd make cash deposits by mail in the names of their agents. Banks will always accept cash deposits, Jessie, even if they don't know where the money comes from. And all that the agents would know is that the money was there. They wouldn't have any idea where it came from."

"Then we'd be looking for a bank where a woman has an account, but never deposits any money in it herself? And if we find one, she'd be the woman we're after?"

"Exactly," Standfield nodded. "And I'd say that when you find her you'll be right close to putting the placer pirates out of business, as well as stopping her from impersonating you."

"Everything you've said makes good sense, Uncle Bert," Jessie agreed.

Standfield said slowly, "Now, Jessie, don't take what I've figured out for holy gospel. A lot of what I've put on this chart is just guesswork, but after the years I've spent learning about banking, it ought to be a pretty well-educated guess."

"Whether you're right or wrong, your well-educated guess has given us a lot more information than we've had before," she told Standfield, taking the chart he handed to her.

"There's one thing more I can do," he went on. "A good friend of mine, Clint Mason, is president of the Farmers and Merchants Bank in Stockton. I'll give you a letter of introduction to him. And I guess you still do some business with my old bank in The City?"

"A fairly substantial amount," Jessie nodded.

"Well, I don't travel the way I used to, so I haven't seen Walt Edmonds for something like two or three years. But if Clint has any doubts about you in spite of my letter, tell him to wire Walt. And that's about all the help I can give you."

"That's a lot more than we've had up to tonight," Jessie told Standfield, kissing him on the cheek. "I'll go tell Ki and Tim what you've uncovered, Uncle Bert. We'll be starting for Stockton tomorrow morning."

"At last we've got something really solid to work on," Jessie said to Ki and Tim as their horses wound down the winding road from the foothills and started across the level delta that lay between them and their destination. "Even if we don't find that mysterious woman in Stockton, we might pick up her trail, which will help us close in on her."

"We've certainly got more information now than we've ever had," Ki agreed. "Mr. Standfield was really helpful."

"He made me feel a lot better when he said if we catch her I might get at least part of my money from her," Tim put in. "I said good-bye to my claim when I saw what that gold dredge had done to it and all the other claims around it."

"Remember what Uncle Bert said, Tim," Jessie cautioned, "about counting chickens before the eggs hatch. Catching up with that woman is one thing, digging out the money she's stolen is going to be a lot harder."

At the first hint of daybreak, Jessie, Ki, and Tim had ridden out of Angels Camp. By midmorning the foothills had been put behind them and they were now crossing the broad alluvial plain east of San Francisco, formed by the juncture of the Sacramento and San Joaquin Rivers.

Croplands stretched to the horizon on both sides of the road, which was dotted with houses and barns of farmers who worked the rich soil. Here and there the slanting rays of late afternoon sunlight glinted from a maze of irrigation ditches and sloughs. There were literally hundreds of these small, sluggish creeks and manmade channels, distributing to the fields the water from scores of rivers and creeks that came together in their courses and joined two great streams or flowed into Suisun Bay and from it to San Francisco Bay and into the Pacific Ocean.

Long before they'd crossed the delta, the sun went down, and as twilight gave way to darkness the final miles of their trip proved to be a frustrating experience. Time after time, they followed what seemed to be a well-used road only to find themselves boxed into a big farm field, unable in the gloom of night to find a bridge that would take them across a wide irrigation ditch or across a creek with banks cut straight down by a farmer who sought to increase the flow of water to his fields.

Already tired by their overlong day in the saddle, Jessie, Ki, and Tim grew even more exhausted as they zigzagged along the road, seeking the bridges that spanned the little watercourses. Their horses soon grew as exhausted as their riders after plodding through the soft, yielding delta soil, and after their first few vain efforts to find a crossing, they began stopping at the nearest farmhouse to ask directions.

Midnight was near before they reached a road that would take them directly to their destination, but soon they saw the lights of Stockton glowing ahead to guide them like a beacon. Weary, they reined in at the first hotel they reached, their exhaustion tempered by the feeling that they'd made a long stride closer to their quarry.

"We'll sleep late tomorrow," Jessie told her companions as they started for their rooms. "The banks won't open until eight or nine o'clock, so there's really no need to be in a hurry."

•　•　•

As they sat eating a late breakfast in the hotel dining room, Jessie said, "There are four banks we'll have to visit. Would it be better for us to go together or split up?"

Tim spoke first. "I don't know about Ki, but after what Mr. Standfield told us, I'd feel a little bit out of place going in and asking a bank to show me their confidential records."

"You know the problem I sometimes have, Jessie," Ki said. "And in farming country like this, I'm sure there are many Oriental field workers."

"You're right, both of you," Jessie nodded. "I'll go to the banks myself, then. And I'll start with the one where Uncle Bert's friend is president."

Clint Mason looked up from the letter Standfield had given Jessie and said, "Bert Standfield doesn't usually write letters like this one, Miss Starbuck. He's told me about the days when he was working with your father, and it's pretty plain he feels you're a very worthy successor to the Starbuck name. I'll do anything I can to help you. What do you need?"

"Information, Mr. Mason," Jessie replied quickly. "From what Uncle—Mr. Standfield, that is—told me, a woman who's been passing herself off as me might have an account in one of the banks here in Stockton. She'd seldom, maybe never, make a deposit in it herself, but the account would receive substantial mail deposits in cash quite regularly."

"And you don't know this mysterious woman's name?" Mason inquired.

Jessie shook her head. "No, but I need to find out what it is so I can stop her from impersonating me."

Mason looked thoughtfully at Jessie for a moment, then asked, "Would this be the same woman I've read about in Clearing-House bulletins who's been buying mining properties and paying for them with fake bank drafts?"

145

Jessie hesitated for only a moment before making up her mind that the time had come to bring the placer pirates into the open. She nodded, and said, "Yes. And since we've started looking for her, we've found out that the claims she swindles the miners out of wind up in the hands of a group of gold dredge operators."

"Miss Starbuck, I'll do anything I can to help you because of Bert's letter and your father's reputation," Mason said. Then he went on, "But if I'll also be helping you to stop those placer pirates from ruining good cropland, I'll put myself at your service with a lot more enthusiasm."

"Thank you," Jessie nodded.

"Now, the only trail you have to this woman is that large cash deposits have been made in her account? Deposits she hasn't made herself?" When Jessie nodded, Mason went on, "Well, I'm sure we have a number of depositors who fit that general description, but very few of them would be women. It shouldn't take me long to find out. If you'll wait just a moment, I'll go talk to my head teller and be right back."

Jessie settled down into her chair, prepared to wait as long as necessary. To her surprise, the banker returned within a very short time, carrying a slip of paper.

"Apparently, the woman you're looking for has created quite a bit of curiosity among our tellers, Miss Starbuck," he said. "Not because of the size of the deposits made to her account, but because of their source."

"What's unusual about that?" Jessie asked.

"Because of the way we get the deposits. Messengers have brought in cash for deposit to her account, but there have also been large drafts deposited in it through cabled funds from the Helvetia Bank in Lausanne, Switzerland, the Dresdener Bank in Leipzig, Germany, Turnbull and Barclay's Bank in Hong Kong, and the Credit Agenais in Paris."

"I can understand why your tellers would be curious,"

146

Jessie said, hiding her thrill of anticipation in her casual tone. "They'd certainly notice anybody who has such wide-spread international connections."

"They're curious for another reason, Miss Starbuck," Mason went on. "Nobody in the bank has ever seen her."

Chapter 14

Jessie's high spirits dropped a notch or two, but again she hid her emotion as she asked Mason, "How is that possible? She must come here to draw money, even if she doesn't make her own deposits."

"About every two or three weeks, a hackman brings us a withdrawal draft. It's always made out to "Bearer," and he has a note from her authorizing us to cash it for him," Mason replied.

"Has she drawn out any money recently?"

"Day before yesterday," the banker nodded. "She withdrew two thousand dollars. That still leaves a balance of more than ten thousand in her account."

"But if she has an account here, surely you have her name and address!" Jessie exclaimed.

"Of course." Mason handed Jessie the slip of paper he'd been holding. "That's the name she was using and the address she gave when her account was opened."

Jessie looked at the slip of paper and read aloud, "Blanche Gregory, 3725 Pacific Avenue."

"That's a section of older houses," Mason volunteered. "It was built up some years ago as a neighborhood of luxury homes, but as the town's grown, a lot of the merchants, who lived there originally, moved closer to the city's center."

"And is this all the information you have on her?" Jessie asked.

"I'm afraid so, Miss Starbuck," the banker replied. "Our records don't show who recommended us or referred her to us or anything of that sort. We don't even know whether she's Miss or Mrs. Gregory. The only other thing I can tell you is that she opened her account with a cash deposit of two thousand dollars."

"When was that, Mr. Mason?"

"Not quite two years ago."

"She must've talked to a clerk or teller or somebody when she opened her account," Jessie wondered.

"Of course," Mason nodded. "But the teller who took care of opening the account doesn't work for us any longer. He quit about six months ago to take a job with a bank in Chicago."

"Don't think I'm being ungrateful, Mr. Mason, when I say I hope this means something," Jessie told Mason. "It's a hundred percent more information than I had before, and I appreciate your help very much."

"I'm sorry I couldn't have done more," Mason told her. "I don't like for our bank to be used by criminals, and now that you've gotten me interested in this mysterious depositor of ours, I'm going to make some more inquiries. Where can I reach you if I find out anything else?"

"I'm stopping at the Beacon Hotel. If you should turn up any additional information, I'd really appreciate you getting in touch with me," Jessie said, standing up. "Right now, I'm going to find Pacific Avenue and see what more I can learn."

Back at the hotel, Jessie passed on to Ki and Tim the scanty bit of information she'd gotten from the banker.

"So since she got money from her bank account the day before yesterday, we can be pretty sure my impersonator is in town," she concluded.

"Then we'll start watching the house on Pacific Avenue, I suppose?" Ki asked.

"Of course. We need to do some scouting first, though. We can't make any plans until we've found out what sort of neighborhood it is, whether there's a place we can use where we won't be noticed. After we've done that, we can decide the best way to go about setting up our observation post."

"If it was left to me, I'd take the bull by the horns and break in her house right now," Tim observed. "Now that we've tracked her this far, I'd sure hate to have that woman get away."

"I'd agree with you, Tim, if she was the only one involved in this," Jessie told him. "But we know now that the woman's not working by herself. We want her, of course, but we also want to get the people behind her."

"Jessie, don't you think it's about time for you to tell me everything that's going on?" Tim asked. "It's not that I object to doing whatever you think is best, but ever since you told me what you did up in Columbia and from the way you and Mr. Standfield acted yesterday, I've been getting downright curious."

After their years of companionship and sharing experiences in their unending battle against the cartel, Jessie and Ki did not need words to agree on a decision. Jessie flicked a quick glance at Ki. He shrugged almost imperceptibly, then moved his head a fraction of an inch, nodding agreement.

"You've been very patient, Tim," Jessie told Moran. "But it's not fair to you to keep you in the dark any longer."

"Well, I've already figured out that you and Ki are up against some sort of gang of these placer pirates," Tim said. "Maybe that's all I need to know, except I'd like for you to say whether or not I'm right."

"You're right, of course," Jessie nodded, relieved that Tim's deductions would spare her the need of going through a complete explanation of the cartel's far-flung criminal

150

activities. She went on quickly, "But the gang's not only interested in gold dredges. It's big and it's spread out into a lot of other things. My father fought it for a long time, before they murdered him. Ki and I are just carrying on his fight."

"And this woman, this Blanche Gregory, she's working for them?" Tim asked.

"I'm sure she is," Jessie replied. "Everything points that way. If you'd rather let Ki and me work by ourselves—"

"Now, hold on!" Tim interrupted indignantly. "I'm not trying to pull out just because I've got into a bigger fight than I looked for when I started out! I'm with you all the way to the end, if you want me to stick."

"Of course, we do, Tim!" Jessie replied. When Tim nodded, she went on, "Good. Now, let's find a livery stable where we can hire a carriage to go out to Pacific Avenue. Tim, do you mind being a coachman for a little while?"

"Certainly not, Jessie," Moran replied. "But why don't we just ride our horses?"

"We'd be too conspicuous on horseback, and I'd just as soon Ki and I stay unseen while we're taking our first look. We'll get a carriage. A brougham will be best; we can look out the windows without being seen from outside."

"If this Blanche Gregory's the woman who claims to be you, she might recognize me, Jessie," Tim frowned.

"I doubt that she'll get a chance to see you at close range. We'll just be riding past the house, this time."

"Let me handle the reins, then," Ki volunteered.

"Perhaps that would be better," Jessie agreed. "Let's go, then. I'm curious to see what we can find out about this mysterious Blanche Gregory."

Pacific Avenue began as a business street at its intersection with Main Street, but after a few blocks it turned into a thoroughfare of expensive homes. These quickly gave way to older homes, many of them converted to boarding houses or flats. Then smaller single-family houses began to appear, and as the brick pavement was replaced by gravel the houses were spaced farther apart.

Long before they reached the address Jessie had been given at the bank, they left the neat square blocks of the city's heart. Here the houses had no apparent rhyme or reason to their spacing and many of them looked dilapidated. At a short distance farther, a levee rose on the right side of the road, which followed the curve of the embankment in a long left-hand curve. Beyond it the houses were spaced even more erratically and stood even farther back from the road. Almost without exception these houses were large and rambling, tree-shaded and bordered with flower gardens, but many of them were vacant and deteriorating. Almost all showed signs of neglect.

"That next house must be the one we're looking for," Jessie said at last, leaning forward to open the little sliding panel between the brougham's body and the driver's seat to tell Ki to hold the horse to a slower pace. "Yes," she went on. "I see the number on that post now."

She turned to gaze fixedly at the large two-story structure they were passing. It stood in a area of tall weeds and neglected undergrowth, which had once been a large flower garden surrounding the dwelling. A number of the windows were shuttered and the shades were drawn on those that were unshuttered. At the back of the house and to one side of it there was a sizable barn. Its doors were only partly closed, but the interior was dark and they could see nothing inside except blackness.

Turning back to Tim, she went on, "I'm not sure that we can do anything here until it's dark."

"I don't think she's at home," Tim said.

"It certainly looks deserted," Jessie agreed. She opened the panel once again and called to Ki, "Drive on until you're sure we're out of sight; then turn around and start back toward town. Tim and I are pretty sure the house is deserted, but we want another look at it."

"I think it is, too," Ki called back. "I don't see smoke coming from any of the chimneys, and it's early enough for a fire still to be burning, if somebody had cooked breakfast."

"On our way back, stop when we can't be seen from the house, then," Jessie told him. "We'd better talk things over before we decide what to do."

Their second slow trip past the house only confirmed their first. When a clump of trees beside the road hid the carriage from the house, Ki pulled off the road into the shelter of the grove and reined in. Jessie and Tim opened the brougham's doors and stepped to the ground as Ki dropped from the high outside seat to join them.

"Do you think we ought to try going in?" Jessie asked them.

"I'm game for whatever you figure we ought to do, Jessie," Tim volunteered. "I'll go with you, or stay here as a sort of watchdog, or anything else you say."

Before Jessie could reply to Tim, Ki said quietly, "Going to the house will not be hard for me, Jessie. Even in daylight, my *ninjutsu* will get me there unseen, but I must go alone."

Cocking his head to one side, Tim asked with a puzzled frown, "What's nin—nin—well, whatever you said. Ki?"

"An ancient art, Tim," Ki answered. "Moving against an enemy without letting him see you."

"Now, hold on!" Tim protested. "That means you'd have to be invisible, and that's nothing but a fairy story, like folks tell kids when they're too young to know any better!"

"I'd believe Ki if I were you, Tim," Jessie said. "He's not boasting."

Tim turned back to say something to Ki and his jaw dropped. Ki had vanished from the spot where he'd been standing a few seconds earlier. Swiveling around, Tim searched the area with his eyes, but there was no sign of Ki.

"Where'd he go?" Tim asked Jessie. "He didn't have time to move very far away. Or did he really do some of that ninjoojoo stuff he was talking about?"

Jessie had not been looking at Ki and had not seen him disappear, but her eyes had been trained by Ki himself to catch the almost imperceptible signs that indicated *ninjutsu* movements. She watched the underbrush between the carriage and the house and picked up the tiny swaying of the tops of the dried rosebushes and thick weeds that told her where Ki was.

"Look at the small dead tree over there," she told Tim as she pointed to a bare leafless young willow that rose above the undergrowth a dozen yards away. "If you watch carefully, you'll see Ki cross that bare spot between the tree and the house."

"How does he do that?" Tim frowned. "That brush is dry as old straw, Jessie. If I was to get into it you could hear me thrashing around for a country mile."

"I told you not to underestimate Ki," Jessie smiled. "Most people do and get surprised—very unpleasantly, I might say."

Tim was silent for a moment, watching the brush for signs of Ki's movements. He saw the tips of a patch of weeds or one of the dead rosebushes twitch occasionally, but could never be quite sure whether the movement was caused by Ki or by the faint breeze that came across the top of the levee. After a moment, he turned to Jessie.

"It's not any of my business," he began, "but I've kept my mouth shut so long my jaws are aching. Can I ask you a personal question, Jessie?"

"Of course. But I'll warn you in advance that if it's too personal I might decide not to answer it."

"It's sorta personal," Tim confessed. "And I hope I won't make you mad. But I can't figure out what it is between you and Ki. Sometimes he acts like he's your hired man, some kind of servant maybe, but other times he acts like there's something more between you. Which is it, Jessie?"

"If you mean a romantic attachment when you say 'something more,' there isn't anything like that between Ki and me, Tim," Jessie replied. "And he's certainly not a servant. It's really a little bit hard for most people to understand."

"Try me and see if I do," Tim suggested.

"Ki's family in Japan is of the very old nobility, bound up in tradition," Jessie explained. "They don't believe in their women marrying outside the aristocracy. Ki's mother married an American, and though her family allowed her to stay with them until Ki was born, they disowned her and cast her out when Ki was a small child. Ki's father died soon afterward, and while his mother lived longer, she also died at an early age."

"But you still haven't answered my question," Tim pointed out when Jessie paused.

"I'm not through yet," she replied. "I had to catch my breath after all that explanation, which you need so you'll understand what happened later."

"I'm sorry, Jessie," Tim apologized. "Go on when you're ready."

"Ki traveled for a while in Japan and Formosa and China, then came to America," Jessie continued. "He was broke and hungry when my father hired him. Surprisingly, they got along very well together and grew to be close friends. They fought side by side against that gang we're after now, and after the gang murdered Alex, Ki stayed to help me. Ki became my right-hand man, just as he'd been Alex's. Now, does that answer your question?"

"I guess it does," Tim nodded. "Thanks for explaining it all to me, Jessie."

"Good," Jessie replied. "Now I just caught a glimpse of Ki going from the barn to the house, so he's on his way back."

"Why, he's walking, just like I would," he exclaimed.

"I'm sure that means there's nobody at home," Jessie said. "And I'm curious to know what he's found out."

Ki emerged from the brush and came toward the wagon a few moments later. He saw Jessie's questioning look and shook his head. He said, "I'm sure there's no one there. I saw a saddle horse in the barn and signs that another horse and carriage are kept there. Since we're not interested in the house as much as we are in questioning the woman who lives in it, I thought we should talk before I tried to get inside."

Nodding thoughtfully, Jessie said, "It was a good decision, Ki. Even with your skill, you might have left signs that someone had broken in."

"What do we do, then?" Tim asked. "Wait until she comes home? We're pretty sure she's in town."

"That would be sensible," Jessie agreed. "We could leave now and come back later. After dark, perhaps."

"Darkness would cover us better," Ki nodded. "And after our hard journey from Angels Camp, I think it would be good for us to rest as much as we can today."

"Yes, you're right about that," Jessie nodded. "We'll go back to the hotel and rest for a while. As soon as it starts getting dark, we'll come back out here and see if we can't put an end to my double's activities."

"That sounds good to me," Tim told them. "I don't mind saying I could stand to catch up on the sleep I lost on the way here." He turned to Ki and went on, "If you'd like for me to take the reins on the way back, I'll sure be glad to. Maybe you and Jessie need to do some talking about tonight."

"A good idea," Ki replied. "While the layout here is still fresh in our minds."

Jessie and Ki were beginning to arrive at a final plan for the evening's action by the time they reached the sweeping curve where the road ran beside the levee. A sudden thumping on the roof of the brougham interrupted them and Ki put his head out the side window to see what Tim's signal meant.

A buggy, its top down, was coming toward them. Ki wasted no time in speaking to Jessie, but dropped quickly to the floor while the two carriages came together. Jessie wasted no time in crouching down on the seat. As the vehicles passed, she got a fleeting glimpse of the two women in the buggy. Aside from a quick glance at the brougham, the women paid no attention to the closed vehicle, but continued their talking without interruption. Jessie raised up and peered through the rear window, but all she could see was the backs of the women's heads.

Within a few minutes the buggy was lost to sight around the curve, Tim reined in, and he leaped from the high seat. He came to the window and exclaimed, "That was her! The woman in that buggy is the one who swindled me out of my claim, Jessie! The one who's using your name!"

"Did she recognize you?" Jessie asked.

"I'm pretty sure she didn't," he replied. "She was too busy talking to the other one, and I saw her in time to duck my head down so she couldn't get a good look at my face."

"We've run into something very interesting here, Jessie," Ki said quietly. "I recognized the other woman. I told you about her in Rough and Ready—Omachi, the one I talked with at the Chinese gambling house."

"Are you sure, Ki?" Jessie frowned. The sixth sense that so often was means of silent communication between her and Ki made any mention of the cartel unnecessary. "You

157

just got one quick look at her as we passed."

"It was all I needed. That's why I dropped to the carriage floor when we passed them. The same thing occurred to me that Tim thought of when he saw the Gregory woman."

"I didn't get a good look at her," Jessie said. "In fact, I couldn't see either of them very clearly."

Ki went on, "If you remember, I was looking out the window before the buggy came abreast of us, and I recognized her at once, even at a distance."

For a moment, Jessie was silent. At last she said slowly, "I think we'd better change our plans. We'll have to keep an eye on that house now and try to find a place where we can overhear what those two are saying."

"That shouldn't be too hard," Ki said. "In this warm weather, they'll probably have some windows open."

"And after what I saw you do today, you can sure get close without them knowing you're there, Ki," Tim put in.

Jessie took up her planning, thinking aloud, speaking slowly. "If they were to leave the house separately, we'd have to split up to follow them, and the carriage would be in our way. We need our horses."

"I can go in, return the carriage to the livery stable, and bring our horses back," Ki suggested. "You and Tim can stay here and keep an eye on them while I'm gone."

"Yes, I suppose that's the best idea," Jessie nodded. "We might need our rifles, too, Ki."

"I know," he said. "I was planning to get them from our rooms."

"You two sure don't waste any time when it comes to figuring things out," Tim said when both Jessie and Ki fell silent. "I guess it was my lucky day when you gave me a chance to throw in with you and Ki, Jessie."

"That's a nice compliment, Tim," Jessie smiled. "Thank you. Now, we'd better start back to that house on foot, and let Ki get on his way to town. We've got a bit of a margin on those two women, and if we're smart we won't lose it!"

Chapter 15

"We'd better get off the road and go through the bushes the rest of the way," Jessie suggested. She angled off their course toward the untended brush and began pushing through the overgrown area between them and their destination. "I can see the corner of the house just ahead."

"I don't know how you do it, but you're not making much more noise than Ki did," Tim remarked after he'd followed Jessie for a dozen yards into the resistant thicket, "I wish I could get through this tangle the way he did. Every move I make starts these weeds rustling."

"We don't have to worry about making noise yet," she reminded him, slackening her pace. "And we've got plenty of time, so the slower we move, the less disturbance we'll make."

"If we're not in a hurry, why don't we circle around the house and come up to it behind the stable, then?" he asked. "That way, we won't have to worry about them spotting us."

"That's a good idea," Jessie agreed. "Let's do it."

Pushing through the head-high tangle surrounding the house was much easier when they could move without the danger of being seen or heard by the women. However, even with the roofs of the house and stable to guide them, making their way through the dense growth took time. A half hour or more went by before Jessie and Tim were able to angle back toward their objective, but Jessie judged the extra time had been worth it, for they emerged from the tall weeds behind the stable, totally shielded from the women inside the house beyond.

"I wish we knew exactly where they were in there," Jessie frowned as they peered cautiously around the corner of the stable at the big silent house, still thirty or forty feet away. "We have to get closer, Tim."

"All we can do is run across that bare stretch," Tim said, nodding toward the strip of graveled soil that lay between the stable and their objective.

"Yes, and we might as well do it. We'll go one at a time, though, so there'll be less chance of being noticed. I'll go first, Tim. Once I'm close enough to the house, we can hug the wall, and they won't be able to see us from the windows. Then we'll work around and hope we find an open window."

"Maybe if we go in opposite directions they won't be so likely to see us," Tim suggested.

"I suppose you're—" Jessie broke off when the thudding of hoofbeats on the graveled road reached their ears. She frowned, then went on, "I'm sure that can't be Ki coming back; it's too soon. We'd better stay where we are until we can move without being seen by those riders."

Their ears attuned to the approaching hoofbeats, Jessie and Tim moved up to the rear corner of the stable and peered around at the road. The horsemen came into view—four men, dressed in city clothing. Instead of going past the house, they reined in their horses as they reached it.

"Uh-uh," Jessie said. "They're stopping. We'll have to wait until they get inside."

By now the riders had left the road and were pulling up in front of the stable. Jessie and Tim could no longer see them, but the men were so close that they heard the creaks of saddleleather when they dismounted.

"Blake, you und Chen vill go vith me," one of them said. His guttural voice emphasized his German accent.

"Sanders, stay here und the buggy guard."

"And miss the fun?" the man addressed as Sanders objected. "I got a special grudge against that snooty slant-eye dame."

"Aw, hell, Gunther!" one of the men broke in. "There's only two women in there and we got 'em two on one. They ain't going to get away!"

"Do not vith me argue, Blake," the man called Gunther said curtly. "Our orders are only to bring der vimmen to der leader in zhape so dey can be kvestioned. Ve are fools if ve do not enchoy dem first."

"Hey, now!" Blake said. "I didn't figure on having a little fun on this job, too."

"Nor did I," another chimed in. From his light high-pitched voice and its unmistakably Oriental intonation, Jessie decided the speaker must be Chen. "There is one—"

"Die bitte Oriental ja. She iss mine first, Chen," Gunther said quickly. "She iss yours ven I finish vith her."

"Come on, Chen," Blake said. "Get that rope off of your saddle-horn and let's go."

"What about me, Gunther?" Sanders asked. "Ain't I gonna get a turn, too?"

"I vill call you ven it is time," Gunther promised. "Now ve must hurry before they look out and zee us."

Jessie had realized by now from what they had seen and heard that the cartel bosses had decided to get rid of Blanche Gregory and Omachi, and that the four men were its hired killers, sent to bring the two women to its secret headquarters for a final session of questioning before their execution.

"We're not the only ones who're going to have trouble," Jessie whispered, the grating footfalls of the men heading for the house drowning her voice.

"Right now we've got enough to suit me," Tim replied.

"That's not what I mean," she told him. "These men are going to take the women away to be murdered."

"What're we going to do, then?" Tim asked.

"Wait until they're inside," Jessie told him. "Then we'll put the guard out of action. That'll make one less to handle after we get in the house. Once we're in there—well, all we can do then it take things as they come."

Jessie slid her Colt from its holster. When Tim saw her move, he drew his own pistol.

"Wait until the ones going inside are busy," Jessie said. "And don't shoot unless you have to; you might hit one of the women."

"What about the fellow they left here?"

"If we're lucky, we can capture him without the ones in the house knowing about it."

"Can we do that and still get to the women in time?" Tim asked. "I sorta hate to think about them—" he paused, trying to think of a less brutal word than rape.

Jessie broke in, "We won't give them that much time, Tim. Now, let me try to draw that guard's attention first. If I can get him to turn around the right way, you can slip up on him from behind." She heard the bang of a house door slamming and went on, "They'll be inside in a second or two. Let's go."

Moving as silently as she could on the hard soil, Jessie stepped quietly around the corner of the stable. Holding her Colt behind her back, she'd taken two steps toward the man called Sanders when her foot slid off a rock and he turned to look at her, his eyes goggling in surprise.

"Who in hell are you?" he asked, staring.

"I might ask you the same thing," Jessie replied. She kept moving slowly as she spoke, circling in a wide arc toward the front of the stable, forcing Sanders to turn to face her.

"It don't make no never-mind who I am," he said, moving

162

a step closer to her. "You got a name, I guess?"

Over Sanders's shoulder, Jessie saw Tim appear from behind the stable and start toward them. She said, "I'm just a friend of Blanche's. But she didn't tell me she was expecting company."

"Now, look here," Sanders began, starting toward Jessie. "I ain't going to—" Loud voices burst from the house and he turned his head involuntarily. His words ended in a grunt when Tim's pistol landed on the crown of his head. Jaw slack, eyes glazing, Sanders crumpled to the ground.

"Quick!" Jessie said to Tim. "Let's drag him into the stable and tie him up. There's sure to be some rope in there."

Inside the stable, Jessie looked around for rope while Tim flopped the unconscious lookout over on his face to ease the job of tying his hands behind his back.

"Here," Jessie said, pulling down a length of light rope from a peg in the wall. "Use this; it'll hold him. Follow me inside when you've got him tied up."

She tossed the rope to Tim and started for the stable door. Thuds and shouts were coming from the house now and a shot rang out. The tinkle of glass breaking drew Jessie's attention to the shuttered window beside the door. It burst open as a bullet tore into it. Jessie veered away from the door and stepped to the broken window to look inside.

She was looking into a kitchen. The wall opposite the window was broken by a door. It stood open, and Jessie saw that the door led into the dining room. She also saw the tip of a rifle muzzle protruding past the jamb and realized that Blanche Gregory and Omachi were putting up their own fight against the attackers, for the three cartel killers were hugging the kitchen wall, where the rifle muzzle could not be brought to bear.

She identified them at a glance. Gunther was a big man with a straggling blond moustache and obviously of Teutonic descent; Chen's Oriental features revealed his identity; and

163

the third man could only be Blake. All three held pistols, but the rifle in the doorway kept them pinned closely to the wall; they could not lean out to sight and shoot without the risk of having their heads blown off by the rifle.

Jessie was in much the same situation. The windowsill was so high that she could not use her revolver's sights, but she raised the weapon above the sill and angled its muzzle downward as best she could. She loosed two quick shots into the kitchen. The unaimed slugs thunked into the wall above the heads of the men who crouched against it.

Before she could trigger off a shot the rifle in the doorway barked again. Its slug ripped into a wall shelf, sending shards of crockery flying. Some of the sharp fragments spattered against the windowframe and Jessie instinctively ducked below the sill. When she peered into the room again she saw that Gunther and Chen had dropped flat and were crawling toward the door where the rifle's muzzle still showed. Blake had retreated to a corner where a slug from the rifle could not reach him. Then Jessie jumped in surprise when a hand closed over the wrist of her gun-hand and Ki spoke from behind her.

"It looks like you're having trouble, Jessie," he said.

Jessie whirled to face him. "Ki!" she gasped. "I don't know when I've been so glad to see you!"

Releasing her wrist, Ki replied, "From what I saw and heard while I was coming up to the house, the cartel's sent some of its men after the women."

"Yes. Tim and I overheard them talking," Jessie replied, speaking quickly. "He's tying up the guard they left to watch their horses. The three others are inside."

"I know how many there are," Ki told her. "They passed me on the road. Luckily, I saw them first and pulled off into the brush. Then I came the rest of the way on foot to avoid noise."

"We'll have to save the women, Ki. They can give us information we need."

"Omachi and the Gregory woman together may well be able to tell us more about the cartel than we could dig up in a year," Ki said and raised himself on tiptoe to look into the kitchen. He started taking a *shuriken* from his sleeve as he turned back to Jessie. "The angle through this window is bad for throwing," he went on. "I'll attack from the door."

As Ki left her side, Jessie looked through the window again. During the short time she and Ki had been talking, the rifle muzzle had disappeared from the inner doorway and the three cartel killers were scuttling crablike toward the opening. She raised her Colt to be ready to join in when Ki launched his attack, and she glanced around. Ki was just disappearing through the back door.

A rifle barked from an upstairs window. Jessie heard Tim's voice raised in a shout of pain. She turned to look and saw him lying on the ground beside Sanders. Whirling to look back into the window, she saw that the cartel men had disappeared through the inner door and Ki was just stepping into the now vacant kitchen.

"Tim's been shot, Ki!" Jessie called. "I've got to go see if he needs help. I'll join you in a minute!"

Ki acknowledged her words with a nod and started toward the inner door.

Jessie turned and ran for the stable. Tim was trying to sit up, a bloodstain spreading over one leg of his trousers.

"Are you all right, Tim?" she asked.

"I hurt a little bit, but all I got was a graze," he replied. He nodded toward Sanders. "He's still alive, though. But I can handle him if he comes to."

"I don't care about him!" Jessie said impatiently. "I asked how you are!"

"I'm all right. Go back to the house and help Ki, Jessie.

165

I'll bind up my leg and take care of this fellow."

"I'll fix him right now," Jessie said. She picked up the rope and with the quick, expert twist of the veteran she'd become by handling a pigging string during the Circle Star branding gathers, she secured the unconscious man's wrists and ankles. She turned to Tim again and said firmly, "Now, I want a look at your leg. Take your pants down, Tim!"

"Now, wait a minute—" he protested.

"Hurry!" Jessie told him. "I've seen men without their breeches on before."

This time, Tim obeyed her. Jessie looked at the bloodstain on the thigh of his knit longjohns and saw that the wound was a shallow crease, the stain still spreading, but very slowly. She whipped her bandanna from the pocket of her own jeans and with a quick flip or two folded it into a layered strip. She pulled the bandanna around the crease, pulled it tight, then secured it with a knot.

"That'll stop you from losing more blood," she said, rising to her feet. "Now, I've got to go back and help Ki."

"I'll be in there with you as soon as I can walk," Tim promised. "Go ahead."

Jessie hurried back to the house and, after a glance in the window showed that the kitchen was empty, went in through the door. She found herself in a small entryway where a staircase led to the upper floor. A shot rang out from somewhere inside, but she was unable to pinpoint its location. Throwing caution aside, Jessie ran through the entry into the kitchen and hurried into the dining room. It was also empty, but she heard the sounds of booted feet thudding above her head.

Glancing around, Jessie saw a door ajar on the opposite side of the room, a stairway rising behind it. In front of her a wide arch opened into the living room, and there was a second stairway at its far end. Making a quick choice, Jessie hurried to the stairway that opened from the dining room.

166

As she started up it, three closely spaced shots sounded from the floor above.

When she reached the head of the stairs she found the door at the top landing was locked. Jessie quickly debated wasting one of her three remaining shells, then fired into the door jamb opposite the lock. The wood splintered as the slug from the Colt tore into it and when Jessie tugged at the knob again the door creaked open. In her desire to reach Ki and help him deal with the three gunmen, Jessie did not hesitate. She yanked the door wide open and with her Colt ready in her hand ran into the room. It was empty.

A muffled gunshot sounded, the flat report of a pistol rather than the sharper high-pitched bark of a rifle, and Jessie glanced quickly around the sparsely furnished room, looking for another door. There were two—one across the room, another at the wall to one side. Her quick glance also showed her that the room had not been used for some time; dust covered the furniture and there was lint on the carpet.

These details registered on Jessie's mind during the few seconds that passed while she debated which door to try. She chose the one across the room, but found it locked and there was no key in the lock. She ran to the second door. It opened and led into a narrow hallway. One end of the hall ended at a blank wall; the other end was open and at one side the newel post of a stairway was visible.

As Jessie ran toward the stairs, she heard the muffled thudding of boots on a carpeted floor. Before she reached the hallway she passed a second door, this one stood open and she glanced into a bedroom. The room was also empty and Jessie did not stop to investigate it, but hurried on toward the stairs. When she got into the open area, she glimpsed the half-visible figure of a body sprawled near the head of the stairwell.

After quickly catching her breath, Jessie moved toward the corpse and sighed with relief when she saw that the body was that of Chen. A doorknob rattled behind her and she twirled around, raising her Colt. Ki came through the door when it opened. He held a *shuriken* in each hand.

"Where did they go?" he asked.

"Downstairs," Jessie replied. "I never did see them, or the women, either."

Indicating Chen's lifeless body, Ki said, "I saw this one as I was coming upstairs; then I investigated this maze of rooms." He was starting down the stairway as he spoke and Jessie followed him.

They reached the living room and hurried across it to the kitchen. Looking out the window, they saw the horses scattered in the expanse of gravel between the house and stable. Gunther was in the buggy with Blanche and Omachi, Blake had caught the reins of one of the skitterish horses and was trying to mount, and Sanders was pursuing another of the animals. Tim was nowhere in sight.

Jessie dropped Sanders with a shot from her Colt. Ki raised his hand to launch a *shuriken,* saw the distance was too great for the star-shaped throwing blade to reach the buggy, and started for the door. The buggy was moving now. Jessie took quick aim at Gunther and fired the last shot in the Colt. She saw the cartel gunman rear back in the seat, but he did not drop the reins.

Ki was racing toward the buggy, trying to get in throwing distance. As fast as he was on his feet, he was no match for the galloping horse. He saw he'd lost the race, turned, and began running back toward Jessie, sliding the *shuriken* back into its sheath as he moved. Jessie dashed for the horse Sanders had been chasing and managed to grab its flying reins before Ki reached her.

"Tim still hasn't shown up!" he said as he vaulted into the saddle and yanked the reins to turn the horse toward the road. "Go back to the hotel after you find him, Jessie. I'll meet you there!"

168

Without waiting for Jessie's reply, Ki kicked the horse into motion and galloped down the graveled road. The buggy was just disappearing around the curve. He hammered the horse's ribs with his heels, trying to urge the animal to move faster. As he reached the end of the long sweeping bend, Ki saw that he was fast overtaking the buggy. He saw Omachi and Blanche flailing at the bulky Gunther, trying to grab the reins, but on the overcrowded buggy seat there was little they could do.

Only a little more than a hundred yards now separated Ki from the buggy, but no matter how hard he drummed his heels into the horse's sides the animal could gallop no faster. He saw Gunther turn in the seat and saw the glinting of blue steel as the cartel killer drew his revolver.

A shot split the air, then another. Omachi tumbled out of the careening buggy and fell in a windmilling of arms and legs to the graveled road. Ki followed the buggy with his eyes for moment and made a quick decision. When he reached Omachi's sprawled motionless form he reined in and dismounted.

Chapter 16

Jessie's fingers were busy reloading her Colt, but her eyes were fixed on Ki as he galloped after the buggy. It was swaying out of sight into the curve of the road, and she watched Ki until he, too, disappeared. She turned back to the house just in time to see Tim limp out the back door.

"Are you all right?" he asked.

"Fine, Tim. How about you?"

"I feel like a fool. I got myself turned around inside that place, and before I could figure out which way to go, everybody had gone outside."

"I can understand that," Jessie nodded. "I was confused myself. That house is like a maze!"

"How about Ki?" Tim asked, looking at Sanders's sprawled form lying in front of the stable.

"He's chasing the buggy. We'll go back to town and meet him at the hotel."

Tim nodded toward the body in front of the stable and asked, "What about him? And the other dead man inside?"

"We'll report them to the town marshal or sheriff or whoever is in charge of local law enforcement when we get back to town," Jessie said quickly. "And we'd better start right away, Tim. Ki said he left the horses up the road a little way. Do you think you can walk to them if you lean on me?"

"I'll manage," he nodded.

"Let's get started, then," Jessie said.

With Tim leaning on her shoulder, they started away from the silent house toward the spot where their horses waited."

Ki was sitting quietly in a secluded corner of the hotel lobby when Jessie and Tim arrived. When he saw them enter, he went to meet them. Jessie looked at him and raised her eyebrows in an unspoken question. He nodded. Jessie turned to Tim.

"You'd better go up to your room and lie down," she told him. "Ki and I need to talk privately for a moment."

"That little scratch I got doesn't bother me, Jessie," Tim protested. "And I want to know what's going on here!"

"You will, as soon as Ki and I finish our talk," Jessie promised. "I'll come up and tell you, and take another look at that wound, too."

Tim looked at though he were going to argue further, but the look in Jessie's eyes held him silent. He nodded and started for the stairs. As soon as he had left, Jessie turned back to Ki.

"Omachi is safe in my room," he said. "She managed to jump out of the buggy. I had no choice but to stop and see if she was still alive, so the man got away with Blanche Gregory."

"I'm sure I hit him with that last shot I fired," Jessie frowned.

"I didn't get close enough to the buggy to see what sort of shape he's in," Ki told her. "That isn't important now, though. Omachi said those men were sent to take her and Blanche Gregory to the cartel's headquarters here in Stockton, and she's promised to tell me where it is. She says it's one of their main operating centers. She's sure we'll find the man and the Gregory woman there."

"Let's don't waste time getting to it, then," Jessie said.

"If it's one of their important hideouts, we should get a lot of other useful information from it, too."

Ki nodded. "I was sure you'd want to attack it. We'll go there as soon as Omachi tells me where it is."

Jessie's eyebrows shot up again, this time in surprise. "She hasn't told you yet?"

"No. She refuses to tell me anything until I get her safely on the next boat to San Francisco."

"Isn't there some way you can get her to talk before that?"

Ki shook his head, then said, "I don't think she'd talk even if I used nerve pressures. You remember what I told you about her. If I try to force her to talk, I'm sure she'd lie to me. Besides, I have no taste for torture. It lowers us to the level of our enemies."

"Did you accept her offer?"

"I had no other choice."

"How long will it take you to get her aboard the boat she wants to take, Ki?" Jessie asked.

"I asked at the hotel desk, and there's one sailing for San Francisco in two hours. That will give me an hour or more to find out all that Omachi knows."

"Keep your promise to her, then," Jessie nodded. "From what you told me about her in Rough and Ready, she certainly must have information we can use."

"I agree," Ki replied. "Look for me in two hours, then."

They walked up the stairs together and separated at the top, Ki going to his room, Jessie heading for her own. She took a roll of bandage linen and scissors as well as a packet of permanganate crystals from her saddlebags and went down the corridor to Tim's room. She rapped lightly on the door and he opened it a crack. She saw that he'd taken off his gunbelt.

"I've come to look at your leg, Tim," she said.

"I hope you'll tell me what you and Ki talked about,

too," he said, swinging the door open to let her enter.

"I'll tell you everything that I can," Jessie equivocated. "But fixing that wound comes first. Now, take your trousers off." She crossed the room to the nightstand, lifted the pitcher that stood in a washbowl, and began pouring water into the bowl. Over her shoulder she said to Tim, "I'll have to soak the leg of your underwear to free it from that dried blood before you can take it off."

Tim had already shed his boots and trousers and was starting to the nightstand. He stared at her and said, "Wait a minute, Jessie! Do you mean I've got to strip naked?"

"I'm afraid so," she nodded.

"Now, Jessie, the way I was brought up—" Tim began.

Jessie broke in. "I know. You were told it's wrong to take off your clothes in front of a woman unless she's your wife."

"I sure was!"

Jessie said, "Tim, I'm the only woman on my ranch in Texas. I've lost track of the number of cowhands who've had to take off their clothes in front of me so I could treat them for a cut or a wound. If you're bashful, wrap one of these towels around you."

Tim went to the washstand and took a towel off its rack. Turning his back to Jessie, he dropped his underwear to his waist and draped a towel around his hips before turning back to face her.

Jessie did not play the game of ignoring his naked body. As she dribbled water from her cupped hand over the blood-stained bandanna, she gazed quite openly at the symmetrical muscles of his shoulders and arms, the matted brown curls on his broad chest that tapered to slim hips and sturdy thighs. When she'd soaked the cloth clinging to his wound, she poured more water into a glass and sifted some of the permanganate crystals into it.

"These will be dissolved by the time we get your un-

173

derwear off," she said. "You'd better sit down on the bed and stretch your leg while I work the cloth out of the dried blood. I don't want to start that wound bleeding again."

Tim sat down and Jessie kneeled beside the bed. She began pulling away the wet cloth of his longjohns from the patch of dried blood that had crusted over the bullet crease. As her warm hands worked along the edges of the soaked cloth, her fingers now and then brushing the smooth warm flesh of Tim's thigh, she saw a bulge forming in the towel and realized that he was beginning an erection. Though in her preoccupation she'd given no thought to the effect her attentions might have on him, she now found his reaction beginning to excite her as well.

Tim shifted his hips, leaning to one side, as he tried to hide the swelling. Jessie had already reached a decision; the same urge that was bringing Tim erect was beginning now to work on her. Quite deliberately, she let her hands touch Tim's thigh more often while she pulled away the temporary bandage and dipped its end into the permanganate solution. Then she dabbed the purplish liquid over the shallow red bullet crease.

"I hope you're just about finished," Tim said. "I'm—"

"You're getting all stirred up," Jessie smiled, looking up at his worried face. "I can see that."

"I'm sorry if I'm embarrassing you, Jessie. I didn't stop to figure—"

"I didn't either. But I'm not a bit embarrassed. Any woman who's honest with herself is pleased when she sees a man getting excited about her."

"You don't mean that you—" He stopped, seeking words.

"Of course, I do. Just let me finish putting this bandage on and I'll prove it to you."

Jessie made short work of winding the bandage around Tim's thigh and tying off. She stood up. The towel was draped like a pyramid now, and Tim was staring at her,

174

frozen motionless, his face a mixture of eagerness and puzzlement. Locking his gaze to her eyes, Jessie kicked off her boots while she unbuckled her gunbelt, and after placing the Colt on the nightstand she made quick work of shedding her clothes.

Tim gasped when he saw her standing naked in front of him, but he still made no move. Jessie's excitement had also grown in the few moments she'd spent undressing. She stepped closer and put a hand on Tim's chest, pushing him onto his back on the bed. With her free hand she pulled the towel away, and before Tim could move or protest she kneeled, straddling him, and sank down on his rigid shaft. Tim raised his hips involuntarily and Jessie sighed softly as she felt him filling her.

For a few moments she did not move, then she began a gentle undulation of her hips, swaying from side to side, revelling in the pleasure of her mounting sensations. She leaned forward, and Tim raised his head to caress her breasts with his lips and tongue—his muscles taut, his hips rising involuntarily now and then in an unconscious effort to penetrate still deeper.

Jessie tightened her inner muscles to increase her pleasure, and when she felt Tim beginning to thrust with a quicker tempo she let herself soar into a quickly peaking climax that arrived as he sighed and fell back. Jessie fell forward, and her lips sought his, and they lay locked in the final rippling moments of their embrace. Then they sagged into the gentle relaxation that comes with the ebbing of total fulfillment.

After several moments had passed during which neither stirred, Jessie raised her head from Tim's shoulder and looked down into his eyes. She said, "I hope you feel as good as I do."

"I don't see how I could feel much better. All I can think about right now is when can we start again."

175

"Any time you're ready," she replied. "We've got another hour together, and I don't want to waste a minute of it."

"That must be the place we're looking for," Ki told Jessie and Tim she reined in and gazed through the darkness at a warehouse's bulk looming against the night sky near Stockton's waterfront district. "It fits the description that Omachi gave me."

"I don't see any lights inside," Jessie said.

"If this gang's as smart as you made it out to be when you told me about them, they'd likely have the windows all boarded up," Tim suggested.

Darkness had fallen by the time Ki had returned to the hotel. They'd eaten a light supper in the hotel dining room while planning their attack. Ki had taken his cue from Jessie. In the complete understanding that existed between them, she'd had no need to give Ki more than a few hints for him to gather that she had adopted Tim's form of reference to the cartel as a gang. He realized quickly that she'd told the young prospector only of the cartel's involvement in the gambling house at Rough and Ready and the gold dredges.

Ki then tailored his account of what Omachi had revealed to match Jessie's limited explanations. He'd said only that Omachi had given him the location of the warehouse and how to reach it. Tim had accepted without questioning what both Jessie and Ki told him, and most of their time at dinner had been spent in planning their sortie on the headquarters.

"We won't gain anything by sitting here," Jessie told her companions decisively. She reached into her saddlebags and took out the lantern she'd bought before they left the downtown district. "Suppose we tether the horses here and see what we'll have to do to get inside that place. I'll wait until we're at the building before I light this."

By the time they'd walked to the warehouse and stopped in the deep blackness beside its wall, their eyes had adjusted to the night. Though they could not make out details, they could see the vague outlines of windows spaced high in the walls and a few paces away a door that broke the plane of the wall.

"All the windows I can see are dark," Ki said.

"Yes. And the door, too," Jessie added. "But let's try it and see if it might be unlocked."

They groped along the wall to the door and Jessie tested its knob. It was locked. She said, "There'll be more doors. Let's walk around the building first, and see if we can't find one that doesn't open onto the street."

Moving cautiously, they started circling the warehouse. They moved through a narrow alley along one side and reached a graveled street behind the building. They saw glints of light shining from cracks around a doorframe and from closed slats of several shuttered windows. Ki pushed gently on the door.

"It's a bit loose," he said in a half whisper. "I think I can break it open with a *ni-dan-geri* kick."

"We aren't likely to find a better place," Jessie told him. "Go ahead, Ki. Tim, we'd better draw now."

Backing away from the door a dozen paces, Ki ran toward it at top speed. When only a yard or so lay between him and the door, he launched himself feet-first at the door. His impetus carried him sailing through the air almost horizontally, and his feet smashed into the door panels with piledriver force. The panels cracked and splintered and what remained of the door burst off its hinges.

Light streamed through the opening and cries of alarmed surprise sounded from inside the building. Ki twisted his supple muscles to throw himself into a midair turn. He landed on all fours and rolled himself erect in time to follow Jessie and Tim as they dashed through the shattered doorway.

Lamps or lanterns on six tables and desks, scattered around

177

the floor, lighted the large room that they entered. Men stood at several of the tables counting money stacked high on their tops, while at the desks others were busy with open ledgers.

They recovered quickly from their surprise. Two of them reached for the revolvers on their tables. Jessie accounted for one of them; Tim for the second.

A pair of the workers nearest Ki had darted toward him while the echoes of the door-smashing still reverberated. He smashed the first to reach him with an *oyayubi-ippon* blow, his stiff folded thumb shattering the fragile bones in the attacker's temple and driving their jagged shards into his brain.

As the first attacker was crumpling to the floor, Ki swung with the momentum of his blow, letting it carry him in a half turn to drop the second man with a *hiji* strike that went home on his assailant's jaw and snapped his spinal cord.

Jessie and Tim had dropped to the floor after their first shots. As the two men still able to move darted from the far side of the huge room, Jessie caught one in the chest with a bullet from her Colt, and when she saw that Tim had missed his shot at the second, she swung her Colt and dropped him as well.

As the reverberations of the gunfire faded into silence, the big room took on the aspects of the morgue it had become. Jessie broke the hush.

"There may be more of them," she warned. "This is a big building."

Neither Tim nor Ki replied. Tim was gazing at the man he'd shot whose mouth lay open frozen in surprise. Ki had his eyes fixed on the door across the spacious room, ready to move if another of the cartel men should appear in the opening. When Jessie felt sure that there was no further danger of an attack, she rose to her feet.

"Tim, if you'll stay here and watch the outside door, Ki

178

and I will look around a bit," she said.

Tim came back to the reality of the present with a start. He started to speak, but his throat was too dry. At last he said as he started to get up, "Sure. I'll stay."

Picking up a lantern from one of the desks, Jessie started toward the door across the silent room. It opened into a door-lined hallway. Ki opened the first door and Jessie held the lantern to shine into the small room beyond. It was an office, furnished only with a large desk and a filing cabinet. They moved to the next and found a shelf-lined chamber piled high with ledgers and taped Manila file folders.

"Records," Jessie said.

"Yes," Ki said. "With names and addresses in them, I'm sure. A real find, Jessie."

Both Jessie and Ki gasped when she opened the last door and saw two corpses propped up against its wall, their glazed eyes staring into nothingness. One was the man they knew only as Gunther. The second was Blanche Gregory.

"I was right about my shot going home," Jessie said soberly as they looked at the bodies, "but I only fired once."

"My guess is that one of the cartel killers was ordered to get rid of the woman," Ki told her. "She knew too much for them to let her stay alive."

"I'm sure you're right," Jessie nodded. "Let's take a look at those ledgers and files, Ki. We'll have to figure out a way to take them back to the Circle Star. They'll be worth their weight in gold to us!"

"A wagon," Ki suggested. "We can go back to the livery stable and rent one."

"I'll take a quick look at them, first," Jessie told him. "And I'm sure by now that nobody's in the building but us, Ki. Suppose you take a quick look around while I glance at some of these papers and ledgers."

Jessie was soon lost in thumbing through the files. As she'd assumed, they were cartel accounts of bribes paid, money received from sales of stolen goods, gambling houses, brothels, and other of the sinister group's depredations.

She'd just begun looking at a ledger devoted to the placer claims that Blanche Gregory had gotten for the cartel through her swindling activities when a shot echoed down the hall. It was followed by a second and then a third. Dropping the ledger and drawing her Colt, Jessie ran toward the big room through which they had entered.

A swirl of smoke greeted her as she reached the door. She burst into the big room. Flames enveloped half the floor area around the door and tongues of fire were beginning to flicker up the walls. Through the smoke she saw Tim, lying on the floor in the room's center, the flames creeping steadily toward him.

Holstering her Colt as she ran, Jessie dashed to Tim. She clenched her hands in the shoulders of his shirt and began dragging him toward the hall. Ki came out of the door just before she reached it and helped her pull Tim to safety in the hall. Only when Jessie released her grip on Tim's shirt did she realize that one hand was wet with blood.

"This hall runs through the building," Ki said, slamming the door that opened into the burning room. "We can get out the other side."

"Let's go quickly, then," Jessie replied. "Tim's wounded, and that fire can't be put out, Ki. This whole building's going to be in flames in another few minutes."

They lifted Tim to carry him between them and hurried down the hall. A key was in the door through which they'd first tried to enter, and in another few seconds they were outside. Flames shot out the door they'd left open as they started carrying Tim toward the horses.

"It's too bad we weren't more cautious," Ki said. "Those records would have gone a long way toward smashing the cartel forever—if we'd been able to get them to the Circle Star."

"Losing them wouldn't have stopped the cartel," Jessie told him. "It would have been a blow they wouldn't have recovered from for a long time. Even if we haven't won the war, we've got a better score than they have."

Just before they reached the horses, Tim stirred, revived by the cool breeze blowing from the river. Jessie and Ki stopped and lowered his feet to the ground. He staggered and they supported him until he could stand alone.

"Two of them," he gasped, when he could talk. "They opened the door and one of them started shooting while the other one dumped a bucket on the floor and tossed a match in it. I couldn't do anything to stop them."

"It's all right, Tim," Jessie assured him. "The important thing is that all of us are out safely."

Tim raised his hand to his wounded shoulder and looked at the blood on it by the light of the flames now bursting through the building's roof.

"I thought I felt funny!" he exclaimed. "I didn't even know I was shot!"

"Don't worry," Jessie said. "When we get back to the hotel I'll come in and put another bandage on you."

By the flickering flames she could see a grin spread over Tim's face. He asked, "Just like the first one?"

"Yes," Jessie nodded. "Just like the first one, but I think it's going to take quite a while longer to finish, this time."